I0575838

Homecoming

ELEANOR WELLS

PUMPKIN CARRIAGE PRESS
Boulder, Colorado

This is a work of fiction. Any resemblance between original characters and real persons, living or dead, is coincidental.

No part of this book may be reproduced in any form or by any electronic or mechanical means, including information storage and retrieval systems, without written permission from the author, except for the use of brief quotations in a book review.

Copyright © 2025 Eleanor Wells

All rights reserved.

FIRST EDITION

Library of Congress Control Number: 2025911139

Ebook ISBN: 979-8-9990404-2-8
Hardcover ISBN: 979-8-9990404-3-5
Paperback ISBN: 979-8-9990404-4-2

Edited by Kaitlynn Flint
Layout by Vellum

Printed in the United States of America by Pumpkin Carriage Press, an imprint of Cinderella Pictures LLC, Boulder, Colorado.

Cover Art by Eleanor Wells
Woman Silhouette in Shadow by Aline Viana Prado sourced from Canva

ALSO BY ELEANOR WELLS

All Our Yesterdays

Fairytale

To my younger self

All that I am or ever hope to be, I owe to my angel mother.

— ABRAHAM LINCOLN

HOMECOMING

IT WAS seven o'clock in the morning, and Rosalie could already tell that it was going to be a hot day. As she entered the living room, the wood floor singed her bare feet. Sean would sleep for another hour, at least. But her mother would be awake soon. Still in her nightgown, she would make breakfast. They would eat in silence, and Alison would go back to her room. Sean would wake up, help himself to leftovers, get dressed, and leave in a hurry to spend the day with Laura. Rosalie would be alone, left to read or listen to the radio or walk over to the diner to get a chocolate shake. Alison kept the record player in her room, and throughout the day, Rosalie would hear the faint sound of Bing Crosby coming from her mother's bedroom, or the soundtrack of *Top Hat*, Fred Astaire's soft voice calling out to his love, to a time now a distant memory.

Rosalie sat down on the couch, rubbed her eyes, and looked out the window. It was Saturday and still of the precious hour before anyone had anywhere to be.

Besides, living in Evanston meant being in an isolated bubble, so close and yet so far from the city all the same.

It was times like these when Rosalie's head was the clearest. In her mind, she formed vivid fantasies of a time and place far from now. She rode the subway in New York City in the finest tailored suit as she carried a leather-bound notepad, on her way to interview important people for a story in the Times.

The past month and a half, since school let out for the summer, and every summer before, had seen many days like this. Rosalie doubted that it being her birthday would make it any different. There was no money to do anything and no one to share it with. No one except Sean. Growing up, he had been there to fill the lonely days. Now, Laura was all that mattered.

Rosalie's eyes drifted to a photograph on the shelf above the radio. It was her favorite, one she stared at often, once so hard she began to notice the blots of ink on the individual fibers of the paper. It was of her parents on their wedding day. Her father was holding her mother in his arms. To them, there was nothing else in the world but each other. Sometimes, Rosalie looked at it long enough that she entered an alternate world where Alison and Jim Hastings were a newlywed couple with the world ahead of them, and there was nothing but their love.

Rosalie stood up and took the picture in her hands. She sat back down with it, continuing her same introspection. Her father looked uncomfortable in his tuxedo.

It was strange to think that she was nearly the age her mother was when she and her father had met. The idea of someone being in love with her was not something that could conceivably be a part of her life. Her mother, who had always been beautiful, was often told she looked like Donna Reed. Now eighteen himself, Sean had grown rather handsome, but Rosalie had never liked the way she looked. Her eyebrows were too thick, her cheeks too puffed out, her mouth too small. Even though she had her mother's sandy hair—she and Sean both did—Alison would tell her how much she looked like her father. She had the same eyes, the same shape of the face.

"You're up early."

Rosalie jolted upward to see her mother standing in the hallway. Three short months ago, Alison had turned thirty-eight. It was on mornings like this when she seemed even older, dressed in a simple nightgown, hair frizzy, bags under her eyes from lack of quality sleep. On the weekends, she had nowhere to go, no reason to pretend that things were better than they really were. "Yeah."

"What are you looking at?"

Rosalie attempted to hide the photo, but Alison had already walked over to the couch and noticed that it was the wedding picture. Alison just smiled as she took it from Rosalie. "I love this picture." For a moment, she stared at it, and she was in this alternate space and time, too. Then she set it down. "I'll make us some breakfast." She kissed her daughter on the forehead and started to walk back towards the kitchen. There was no indication that she was aware that it was her daughter's birthday. It would come to her later in the day, Rosalie thought. She sat there on the couch and sighed.

Alison and Rosalie had just sat down to breakfast—bacon, eggs, and toast—when Sean emerged, still in his pajamas. Alison turned to her son. "There's eggs and bacon on the stove," she said.

"Coffee?" Sean muttered.

Alison nodded. Soon, Sean had sat down next to them at the table, his plate piled high with food. He began to eat, and he turned to Rosalie. "I was thinking," he said, "that I would take you into the city."

Rosalie took a moment to process. She was surprised but pleased at the prospect of spending time with her brother. "Sure," she said.

Alison just smiled.

AFTER BREAKFAST, ROSALIE AND SEAN GOT READY and left within the hour. On the train, they said nothing. Rosalie was afraid of saying the wrong thing, so she said nothing at all. It had been so long since Sean had asked her if she wanted to do anything, and she didn't want to mess this up, but it seemed as though Sean had nothing to say to her either.

When they arrived, Sean bought them both vanilla ice cream cones, and they ate them in a shaded spot in Grant Park. It had been two weeks since the Fourth of July, and yet the city was still packed with people. Rosalie ate her ice cream cone, searching desperately for something, *anything* to say.

"So, what do you want to do today?" Sean finally asked her.

"I don't know," Rosalie said.

They'd been a family once, but that was a very long time ago. She longed to feel it again, and maybe there was some part of Sean that wanted to feel it too. The fact that they were together now, on her birthday, was something. Still, he had yet to say it. Two words. *Happy birthday.* "I was thinking we could go see *Treasure Island*. We're not far from Uptown."

"Sure," Rosalie said. Pirates would be fine. Rosalie had read the book once, and it hadn't left much of an impression on her, but maybe doing something Sean wanted to do would make him happy. Break him out of the sour mood he always seemed to be in.

They finished their ice cream, got up, and began to walk. They were on Michigan Avenue now, the hub of the city. Rosalie liked Chicago, but to her, it always seemed to be a lesser version of New York. At least, New York, the way Rosalie always remembered it. New York had her father.

Finally, as they walked, Sean acknowledged what they'd been dancing around the entire day. "Is there anything you want for your birthday?"

Rosalie said nothing.

"I don't have a ton of money to spend," Sean said. "But I can buy you something." Rosalie stared at her brother, dumbfounded. It had been a while, a long while, since she'd gotten any kind of present. For her birthday or for Christmas. It wasn't something their family had talked about in a long while. "Don't just look at me."

"Maybe, after the movie, we could stop by a book-store?" Rosalie said. "I'd like a new book."

"Sure," Sean replied.

They walked for a little while longer in silence.

THE THEATER WAS FAIRLY CROWDED. AFTER ALL, IT was a Saturday and the movie had only been out for a few days. It was fine. Nothing spectacular.

Afterwards, it was more of the same.

"What did you think?" Sean asked her.

"Really good," Rosalie said.

Somehow, it had gotten even hotter. It was almost too hot to be comfortable. Not that it would be any more comfortable at home. They didn't have air conditioning; that was only for rich people to afford, rich people with their apartments on Michigan Avenue. And if Rosalie ever complained, her mother would always bring up the Depression, about how good Rosalie and Sean had it compared to what she and their father went through when they were just starting out.

Afterwards, they stopped by the bookstore and Sean bought her *The Grapes of Wrath*. She'd never read it before, but she vaguely remembered her father talking about the movie once. People often called him Tom Joad, and with good reason—in his younger pictures, with his shirt, overalls, and flat cap, he bore an uncanny resemblance to Henry Fonda.

Before they knew it, they were on the train back

home, without having accomplished much of anything at all. *I can't even talk to my own brother,* she thought. *Why can't I talk to my own brother? It wasn't always like this.* When they got back, Alison must have been lying down, because she was nowhere in sight. Sean went to his room, and Rosalie went to hers.

2

THE REST of the summer dragged on, filled with many long, lonely days. Laura came over for dinner one night at the end of July. She'd enrolled in a summer painting class at Columbia College Chicago and had a portfolio of pieces with her. Rosalie waited impatiently with her and Sean in the living room for Alison to finish cooking. They were ignoring her, whispering about the inevitable day her art would be in galleries across the world.

Laura had always been plain-looking—she was thin and lanky with frizzy blonde hair and flat features. She'd been Sean's steady for nearly four years, and Rosalie still felt like she didn't really know her brother's girlfriend. Things were simpler when she wasn't around. She saw more of her brother before Laura. She confided in him more, and he confided in her. Rosalie always got the impression that Laura preferred she was not around, so that she could have Sean all to herself.

Alison announced dinner, and the three of them sat down at the dining table. Shortly thereafter, they all began to eat. It was a quiet, rather awkward dinner. There was a lull in the meal, at which point Sean took Laura's hand, and it got very quiet.

"We have something that we would like to announce," Laura said.

Alison and Rosalie both turned to them. Sean spoke. "We talked it over this afternoon. We're going to be married."

Rosalie felt numb. She already saw how it was going to go. They would marry. Move into their own apartment. Start their own life. Rosalie would be left with her mother, and she would be even more alone. Alison didn't seem thrilled either, but still, she began to ask questions. About the wedding. If they had a plan. Without a word, Rosalie got up from the table, walked into her room, and slammed the door. She could feel their eyes on her, but she didn't care.

The tears came quickly. The quiet of her room was overwhelming, but it didn't last long. There was a loud knock at her door. "Yes?"

Her brother spoke. "It's me."

"Come in."

Sean's face, masked by the shadows, was tight. Rosalie sat up as he approached her bed. "What was that about?" he demanded.

Rosalie shrugged.

"You embarrassed me," he said. He breathed out. He was clearly angry, and Rosalie found herself afraid of what he might do. But after a moment, he seemed to calm down, and he sat on the bed next to his sister. Looked at her. "Aren't you happy?"

For a moment, Rosalie looked down at the floor. Yes, she supposed she wanted Sean to be happy. If they were happy and sure that getting married was the right thing, that was most important. Still, she asked, "Are you sure she's the one?"

"I'm sure," Sean responded.

"Then you have my blessing."

Sean was less tense now, and he looked at Rosalie in such a way that she thought that they might hug. She realized that she didn't remember the last time that they had. But he simply stood up, pursed his lips, and hesitated at the doorway. "Good night, Rosalie," he said before he left.

It was only about seven-thirty at night, not nearly time for bed, and Rosalie wasn't the slightest bit tired. But Sean and Laura went out for milkshakes and to a movie, ignoring Alison's advice that if they were going to get married and move into their own home, they needed to be more careful about how they spent their money. Shortly afterward, Alison summoned Rosalie into the kitchen to do the dishes. Alison sat on the couch, knitting a new scarf for the winter, even though it was July.

Rosalie scanned through the channels on the radio before she heard Walt Disney's voice, and stopped. He was being interviewed about the recent success of *Cinderella*, a film she had yet to see, and the production of the upcoming *Alice in Wonderland*. It was due to come out the following summer. Rosalie would be seventeen by then, which seemed so far away.

"Didn't you say you read *Alice in Wonderland?*" Rosalie asked.

There was no response.

"Mom?"

Alison looked up from her knitting.

"Didn't you say you read *Alice in Wonderland* growing up?"

"Oh, yes, my mother had it in the house."

"Disney's doing a film," Rosalie said. Even though it was clear her mother was not interested, she was trying desperately to keep the conversation going.

"That's nice," Alison responded. Then it was silent again. Rosalie sighed and changed the channel on the radio again. This time, to music. By chance, it was Bing Crosby, her mother's favorite. While Alison did continue to knit, Rosalie noticed her mother smile slightly.

After what seemed like a long time, Alison spoke. "So, what do you think?"

"About what?"

"Sean and Laura."

Rosalie had no idea how to respond. She didn't want to talk about it, not now, and especially not with her mother. So she merely shrugged.

"I don't think he's ready."

"Weren't you his age when you married Dad?"

Alison got defensive. "Yes, but that was different. We all had it hard back then. We knew what it meant to really work for something. To make sacrifices."

Rosalie said nothing, and before long, she'd changed

into her pajamas and retreated into her room for the night.

She lay awake for what felt like an eternity. At some point, she heard Sean come back, but she stayed in bed, not feeling very much like talking.

DECEMBER WOULD MARK SEVEN YEARS SINCE THEIR father had been gone and eight since they'd all been a family. On their last perfect day together, all the way back in 1942, Jim Hastings had taken his children, then eight and ten, sledding. Alison had stayed home to get dinner ready. It was nearing dusk, and there had recently been a fresh snowfall that had transformed the nearby public park into a winter wonderland.

It was half her life ago, but Rosalie could still make out her father's form at the bottom of the hill. His wide eyes watching. The warmth that radiated from him as he called out to tell her that she could do it. As Rosalie stood at the top, shaking beside her sled, Sean was beside their father, squirmy and impatient. Jim turned to Sean and said something that Rosalie couldn't quite make out, but it seemed to calm him down.

"Rosalie?" Jim called.

Rosalie was frozen still. The hill seemed so steep, her father so distant. The sun had gone down, and it was beginning to grow dark. Soon it would be black and cold. She started to cry.

"Oh, Rosalie," muttered Jim before he climbed up the hill. He got on his knee so he was eye to eye with his daughter. "What's the matter?"

"I'm scared," she responded.

"Why are you scared?" He responded calmly.

"It's so high," she said.

Jim looked down at the hill and managed a smile. "Well, you've never done it by yourself before, right? It'll be just like when I went down with you."

Rosalie shook her head.

"New things are scary. But you know what?" He looked at her lovingly. "They get less scary after you do them."

Rosalie listened.

"Now, I don't know about you, but I'm getting hungry and I'm sure Mommy's got a tasty dinner cooking at home," he said. "But, if you don't want to go, we can let your brother go down one more time, and then we can go home." He waited for Rosalie's response.

"I want to go."

Jim smiled widely. "I was hoping you'd say that. Want me to give you a push?"

Rosalie nodded. She climbed onto the sled, still scared but a little excited. Jim counted down. He pushed and ran down to meet his daughter, who leapt into his arms with a smile on her face at the bottom. Laughing.

"Was that fun?"

Rosalie nodded. They turned to Sean, and Jim gave him a nod. He darted up the hill and went down himself. Once they were all at the bottom, Jim turned to his two children and hugged them tightly.

It was on lonely nights like this that Rosalie thought she could still feel the warmth of his grasp.

3

ROSALIE NEVER BROUGHT up her father unless her mother did first. The reason for this was that she was never sure how Alison would react when he was mentioned. Sometimes she was wistful, romantic, longing, and even happy. Other times, she shut down completely.

As July became August, Rosalie found herself wanting to talk about her father, but not wanting to cross an awkward line that she couldn't take back. But one morning, she and her mother were both in the kitchen. Sean was still living there, but he was often out for wedding planning; he and Laura had a date set for the end of the month. Her mother was reading the paper while Rosalie did the dishes. The radio was on, and both were half listening. It was some sort of lifestyle segment, talking about all of the fun ways that families could spend their summer. They were discussing a campground up in Wisconsin, by Lake Superior.

"Did I ever tell you about the time I visited your father when he was working for the CCC?" Alison said.

"I don't think so," Rosalie responded.

A smile crept onto Alison's face. "You weren't born yet. Sean was maybe two? We'd just gotten married, and your father got the job with the CCC. We really needed the money, but it was hard, being away from him. We drove out, and Sean saw your father and ran straight towards him. And he kept shouting, 'That's my daddy!'"

"Did I ever do anything like that when I was younger?"

Alison laughed. "Not that I can think of."

Rosalie looked at her mother, still distant. Somewhere, she found the courage to ask what she wanted to ask. "Mom," she said. "How did you and Dad fall in love?"

"At the soup kitchen," Alison said, knowing Rosalie had heard the basics of the story before. But, as a child, she'd been given a simplified version. Now that she was older, Rosalie realized she didn't know any other specifics.

"But how did you fall in love?"

"We never told you?"

"I don't think so."

Alison took a deep breath. "Well, I was living with my parents, your grandparents, and we'd just lost our house. Your aunt Violet had a small apartment with your uncle Eric, and we all moved in. Five of us in a space meant for two. But we did what we had to do." Her eyes were far away. She was reliving that time, if only for a moment.

"One day, everyone else was occupied, so I went to the soup kitchen by myself. Your father was in line in front of me. He said hello, and we got to talking from there. I told him about the apple pie that I liked from the bakery. But we just talked. Nothing more." Alison paused to laugh. "I suppose I was oblivious, because your father told me later he knew then I was the woman he was going to marry. I found I would look forward to going to the soup kitchen just so I'd be able to see him. We'd known each other for about a month, gotten rather close, and on Thanksgiving, he brought me the apple pie. I found out he'd saved a bit of his wages for weeks to do it. And that's when I knew too."

Rosalie imagined the scene in her head. A wide-eyed, sandy-haired girl, somewhat out of place in the dirt and grime. Her father, overalls, flat cap, unkempt dark hair, but still the same kind face. Two young people about to fall in love, the world ahead of them. As far as Rosalie knew, there had been no one before Jim, and there had certainly been no one after. As far as Alison was concerned, he was it, and to go with anyone else would feel like cheating. Rosalie wondered if she'd ever have a love like that.

Sean thought he did with Laura, but at least to Rosalie, it didn't seem to be the same.

But that didn't stop the wedding, a small affair with only a handful of guests. They'd found a small apartment on the South Side, which they'd secured with help from Laura's parents, and they'd moved into shortly thereafter. Sean's summer work as a lifeguard had ended and he was without any prospects, to which Alison had said, "you're on your own now. You're going to have to figure it out." The goal was to sell Laura's paintings and make enough money to earn a decent living, which the two seemed determined to do.

The night before, as he'd packed up the last of his things, Sean had sensed Rosalie's uneasiness. "I'm only a phone call and a train ride away," he'd told her. And yet, a month had passed, Rosalie and Alison alone, waiting out the dull, bored quiet of summer, where neither sibling spoke. Every time Rosalie thought about picking up the phone, something inside told her not to. *He's busy. He doesn't have time for me.* He'd called to tell them that he'd found steady work with a construction company, but the conversation had not lasted any longer than that.

As the summer wound down, Rosalie began to think about returning to school. She enjoyed class, and even though she didn't have any real friends to speak of, it was better than being at home. Besides, she only had two more years. After, the future was wide open. She could go back east, to New York, go to Barnard. Maybe Radcliffe in Boston. But Barnard was her top choice. She could meet new people. Start her life over. Maybe even have a family of her own.

IT WAS ANOTHER HOT, BORING DAY WHEN ROSALIE decided to walk to the diner for a chocolate shake. While she didn't yet have a job, her mother sometimes gave her extra pocket money. She had been sitting in the living room, listening to the radio, but she wasn't able to find a station that she wanted to listen to. Her mom had to have been resting, because when Rosalie called out to her, she didn't answer. So she wrote a note, took her purse, and made the fifteen-minute walk over.

Rosalie always felt somewhat out of place amidst the bright colors and sounds of Chicago's diners. But this one, here in Evanston, was her favorite. The servers were nice, and the chocolate shakes were heavenly. On this particular day, it was filled with couples or groups of friends. By herself, Rosalie felt awkward and out of place as she waited in line. She thought maybe she would get it to go, walk back home, find something to read or listen to on the radio that she didn't hate. That was when she saw Mark Copeland. His dark hair was slicked back from his face and he was dressed in a dark shirt and light pants that it was still too hot for. His blue eyes gazed at the wall beside him. They'd never actually spoken, but she saw him often in the halls. He was a year above her, this year's editor in chief of the school paper. He was eating lunch, reading something, it looked like. She bit her lip, finding she was starting to shake as she approached the counter.

As she moved closer, she found Mark's eyes were on hers as well. Nervous, she stared at him, unsure of what to say, so she said nothing. He laughed nervously.

"We go to school together," Rosalie finally said.

"Right," he responded, taking a minute to place her. "You're Sean Hastings's sister, right?"

"Yeah, I am."

"Awesome," he said, before going back to his book. The conversation was clearly over but Rosalie still found her gaze cast towards him and the empty seat at his side. She saw a few people in line looking at her, and realized it was her turn before she approached the counter.

"Chocolate shake, please," she said. Once she paid, she lingered beside Mark, scanning the room. There were a few open places she could sit scattered throughout. She was about to find one on the other end of the diner when she heard him mumble something.

"What was that?" she asked.

"Do you want to sit here?" he said, gesturing to the empty seat at his side.

Rosalie shook.

"No sweat if you're waiting on someone."

In response, Rosalie slid into the seat, nervously twiddling her thumbs as she turned away from Mark. She was blushing bright red and didn't want him to see.

"What's your name again?" he asked.

"Rosalie."

"I'm Mark."

A waitress then approached and gave her the shake. Rosalie began to sip it. Mark looked over at her. "That looks delicious."

"These are my favorite."

"Maybe I'll try one next time," he said with a smile.

"What are you reading?" Rosalie asked.

Mark turned over his book cover. *The Great Gatsby.* Rosalie had never read it, but she'd heard good things. "How is it?"

"I've read it before. It's pretty good."

With the conversation dying out, Rosalie changed

the subject. "Are you excited to go back to school next week?" she asked. She felt so awkward, so clumsy, and a million thoughts were swirling through her head. *He thinks you're weird. Stop acting weird.*

Mark shrugged. "Eh." After a laugh, he added, "About as excited as you can be."

"So," Rosalie said. "I heard you're going to be editor in chief of the paper this year."

He nodded. "Right."

"I was wondering, well, if I might be able to join?"

"Sure," he said. "Everyone's welcome. We just need a writing sample, but you can bring that to our first meeting. It'll be Tuesday. After school."

"The first day?" Rosalie said.

"Sure," Mark replied. "We want to get the ball rolling, I guess."

"Alright. I suppose I haven't written anything that would be suitable," Rosalie admitted. It was true. She'd written a lot more when she was younger. Fantasy stories about princesses and mermaids, ones she illustrated herself. After her father died, she stopped. But in the past few years, she'd become interested in it again. In the news. In history. In ways to immortalize singular moments of time. But she had no audience, no one to read her work. She had a lot of ideas, but nothing she'd committed to the page.

"Well," Mark said. "You have a week."

"I guess I do," she said.

"You like writing?" he asked.

"Sure," she said. "I suppose I've always wanted to be

a writer. I used to write more fiction, but now I think I want to be a reporter."

"Really? That's interesting." He paused. "I guess I've never met any girls who have wanted to do that."

Rosalie shrugged. She rarely, if ever, thought about her gender as a barrier to her career. Her father used to tell her that she could be anything she wanted to be, so she always believed it.

By this time, Mark was done with his lunch, and he took his book and stood up. "Well, Rosalie, I've got to get going. But, see you next week I guess, right?"

She nodded. "Right."

Rosalie watched as he left, finishing the rest of her shake in a sort of suspended animation.

That night, Rosalie lay awake in bed, unable to stop thinking about Mark. She was going to join the paper, so they would interact regularly. Of course, she wasn't only joining for him. And he was certainly more than a handsome face. He was smart, and he cared about the same things that she did. Would this be it for her, the time she finally stopped being lonely? Maybe Mark would ask her out on a date, kiss her the way she only knew from movies, and tell her that he loved her. She told herself to calm down. It was far too early for any of that. Besides, if she was going to join the newspaper, she was going to have to write an article first. She had five days left of vacation to think of something.

Rosalie awoke in the middle of the night to use the bathroom after a vivid dream. She had been at a train station. It seemed to be Union Station. It wasn't explicit, but that was what she had sensed, even though she had never actually been. Rosalie sensed she was older from the way she dressed and carried herself. She had a train to catch, but was running late. It was busy, and she couldn't find her gate, for it hadn't been printed on her ticket. Then, she woke, lying in her own bed without any resolution.

She got up to go to the bathroom, and as she started walking back to her room, she felt an acute sense of being awake and figured that she was going to have trouble falling asleep again. As Rosalie passed her mother's room, she thought she heard stirring. Then, the sound of crying. She was definitely awake, and she was crying. Rosalie paused, wondering if she ought to do something. She vividly remembered a similar scenario once, after they had just moved to Chicago.

They'd only been in their apartment for a few weeks, and it was still filled with boxes. It was springtime. May 8th, 1945. VE Day. She still heard the voice of the radio announcer. *Germany has surrendered unconditionally to the Allied Powers, led by General Eisenhower...*

She and her mother and Sean had been sitting on the couch. Rosalie remembered her mother's face. Elation that quickly turned into uncontrolled sobbing and then nothing. Her walking silently to her bedroom. Later that night, Alison had not emerged, and Sean and Rosalie were beginning to get hungry. Sean had gone to check on her, and when he returned to the living room, he told Rosalie that Alison had told him to make peanut butter and jelly sandwiches.

"Want to get a hot dog?" Sean asked. Rosalie

nodded, and they took the train into the city. They got their hot dogs from a stand and sat on top of a hemispherical jungle gym in a park, looking up at the sky. It was a warm night, and they sat there for a while, not really talking. Then, Rosalie turned to her brother.

"Do you think Mommy will ever be happy again?"

Sean didn't answer.

Even though they had won the war, and many soldiers would be coming home, there was one who wouldn't be.

They'd gotten the telegram two days before Christmas. Their father had been away for a year at that point, and the last correspondence from him had been a month earlier. He was tired, and he missed them all terribly. He didn't know when he was going to be able to come home, but he hoped it would be soon. And although he wouldn't be able to make Christmas, he would be with them in spirit. Still, they'd done it the way they always had. Gotten the tree from the tree farm. Brought down the box of decorations. Listened to the classics on the radio. Snow fell softly outside against the black night. Rosalie remembered it so vividly she could hear the music playing, feel the texture of the ornaments in her hands, see the pale yellow of their walls, taste the roast Alison had made for dinner. It was almost perfect. The only thing missing was Jim.

The doorbell rang. Alison set down her ornament. "I'll get it," she told her children. She opened the door. Sean and Rosalie both saw the Western Union man hand Alison the telegram and quickly walk away. They saw her drop it into the snow and weakly pick it up. She closed the door, walked over to her children, and held them tightly as she sobbed.

4

BEFORE LONG, the first day of school had come. Rosalie received a rare gift from her mother—a new dress—for the occasion. "For your birthday," Alison explained.

She'd always worn her hair back in a ponytail, but that morning, staring at her reflection in the white and blue floral sleeveless number, she decided to leave it down. She looked at herself in the mirror, content. With her new look, she seemed more poised, more sure of herself. Fifteen year old Rosalie was still a child, too nervous to talk to people. Now, sixteen year old Rosalie looked like she could go places. Like she could be a part of the school paper and talk to people without overanalyzing everything they said.

She had a good feeling about this year. It was a fresh start, and it was going to be different. She kept her notebooks safely in her bag, and in one of them was an article she had written the night before about the Korean War. It wasn't her best, but she only hoped Mark would like it enough.

As she walked down the hallway, getting ready to leave, she heard her mother stirring in her room and realized she had not yet left for work. Alison was a secretary at a local paper company. She never talked about it much.

Rosalie knocked on the door.

"Mom?" she asked.

"Come in," Alison said.

Rosalie opened the door. She was sitting in front of her vanity, humming to herself as she brushed her hair. Still in her nightgown.

"You look very pretty," Alison said.

"Don't you have work?" Rosalie asked.

"No, I quit," she said matter-of-factly.

"When?"

"This morning."

"Why?"

"I didn't want to work there anymore," Alison said with a smile—a rare expression Rosalie had not seen in a while on her mother's face.

"What about money?"

"I'll find another job. I'm not worried about it."

This whole encounter was much too bizarre for Rosalie to deal with. "I have to go to school," she said before shutting the door.

At lunch, Rosalie took her usual seat by herself. A couple of people who she hadn't seen since summer had said hello to her.. She was friendly with a lot of people but real friends with no one. So far, the morning had been alright. She was most looking forward to History and English, which would be in the afternoon. And of course, after school, when the paper would meet.

Just then, she caught eyes with Mark walking with his lunch tray across the cafeteria. He saw her looking and smiled at her. "Are you waiting on anyone?" he asked.

Rosalie shook her head, and Mark gestured for her to take her lunch and come over. She could scarcely believe it, and she sat there dumbfounded for a moment. When she finally got her things together, he laughed. Still, Rosalie said nothing, and they continued walking to the other end of the cafeteria. "How's your first day so far?" Rosalie asked when she could speak.

"It's been just fine," he responded.

They sat at a table of twelfth grade boys whom Rosalie knew by face but not by name. Mark introduced her, but she forgot most of their names in a second. While they mostly waved and went back to their conversations, there was one, a boy with red hair and freckles, whose gaze lingered on Rosalie's from across the table. He reached over and they shook hands.

"Pleasure, I'm Joe," he said.

"Rosalie," she muttered, immediately turning back to Mark. "Did you know my brother well?"

Mark shook his head. "We did have English together last year."

Rosalie laughed. "And how was that?"

Mark looked at her for a moment, as if he didn't know how to respond. "I enjoyed it. Read a lot of good books. And I like your brother."

"He got married," she said.

"To Laura Martin?" Joe cut in.

Rosalie nodded. Mark laughed. A couple of the surrounding boys heard and they joined in the chorus.

Rosalie blushed, noticing Joe's eyes were still on her. Mark caught her attention then. "So, Rosalie, what do you want to do after high school?"

"I want to go to New York to become a reporter," she responded confidently. "I'd like to go to college, too. Maybe Barnard."

Mark smiled. "I'm hoping to get into Columbia. I've always wanted to live in New York."

"I grew up there," Rosalie said.

Mark's eyes widened. "Really?"

"My parents are both from there. We moved after my dad died."

"Oh. I'm sorry to hear that."

Rosalie took a deep breath. "I was really young when it happened. But I still miss New York."

Mark's eyes started to wander, and Rosalie wondered if she'd been too forward in mentioning her dad. Even though she'd thought about him constantly, she had to remember this was only the second time that they'd spoken. Still, the rest of their lunch went by normally, and they ended up chatting about everything and anything. It was nice. It had been far too long since she'd really talked to someone. Maybe this was what it was like to not have a hole in your heart so deep you wondered if there was something wrong with you. It brought about a sort of warmth, and she hoped that it was here to stay.

The rest of the day had passed uneventfully, but at

the school paper meeting, Mark had liked her article. She was the only girl, but that didn't matter to her.

She came home that evening with a smile on her face. Her mother was sitting on the couch, paging through Malone's fall catalog. The delectable scent of something baking wafted out from the kitchen.

"Hi, Mom," she said.

"Hello," Alison responded. She seemed to be in a good mood, and Rosalie remembered what had slipped her mind earlier that day, that Alison had suddenly quit her job. Rosalie didn't know what to say, so she said nothing about it. She trusted that her mother would find another one before things got too difficult for the two of them again. Rosalie wished that she were old enough to work. Of course, she was still far too young to be a real journalist, but she wanted any sort of job. Something where she could get out of the house and earn money of her own.

Then, Rosalie saw the cookies before her mother pointed them out. Alison smiled. "I made chocolate chip cookies."

Rosalie smiled and walked over to the kitchen counter. She got herself a plate and a glass of milk and went to sit by her mother. Because Alison was rarely in a good mood, she wanted to make the most of it while she could.

Her mother smiled as she bit into the cookie. It was still warm, and she didn't know if there was another sensation that was quite as comforting. Not since the cinnamon rolls her mother used to make on Christmas morning, anyway.

"Mom?" Rosalie asked.

"Yes?"

"Why don't we go to a movie?"

"I'd like that," Alison said. "Why don't you check the paper?"

Rosalie obliged. Her mother used to take her and Sean to the movies often. And her father loved the movies too. It was one of their favorite pastimes as a family, but they hadn't gone since Fred Astaire and Ginger Rogers's *The Barkleys of Broadway* the year before. Her favorite movie was *The Best Years of Our Lives*. It always made her a little sad because she knew her father hadn't returned home from the war, but she liked it nonetheless. She didn't talk about it often because the day after they'd gone to see it, her mother had seemed especially depressed for the rest of the week. But maybe one day she'd have the patience and discipline to do her hair like Teresa Wright.

Rosalie saw a listing for Disney's *Cinderella*. That would be perfect. Her mother agreed.

They were relatively silent on the train over, and Rosalie found herself racking her brain for something to say. Why was she so bad at talking to people? Sean wasn't like that. He always had friends. And Laura wasn't like that either. Neither was her mother, whenever she did feel like being sociable with people. She then thought about why she was upset when Sean had moved out and gotten married. He was her only friend. Maybe she needed to make more. Because she couldn't think of anything to say, for the rest of the train ride over, she decided to people-watch. The train was less crowded than she thought it ought to be for a weekday evening, but it was peaceful. Everyone minding their own business. Most were reading the paper.

They got to the theater, and Rosalie was hungry for some candy, but Alison declined to buy either of them snacks. Before the movie began, still relatively crowded for a film that had been out for a while, there was a newsreel about the ongoing conflict in Korea. The absurd humor of the Donald Duck cartoon that followed it clashed heavily in tone. But wasn't that why people went to the movies? To forget?

Then, the film began, and Rosalie was swept up in it the way she always had been on their childhood trips to the theater.

It was Disney's best one yet.

Alison didn't have much to say about the film on the ride home, only "I'm never going to remarry." Rosalie said nothing. Her mother's lack of dating history in the past seven years was a conscious choice. Still, Rosalie wondered if another man would help Alison not feel as lonely.

Once they got home, Rosalie retreated into her room to read *The Grapes of Wrath*. As she read about the Joads and their unending quest for a better life, she tried to feel more connected to her father. In a way, it did, but knowing that his time was gone made her sad. Something else happened, though. The longer she read, the more she forgot about her own life. So, she continued, letting the hours pass until she was tired enough to go to sleep.

She awoke at two o'clock in the morning after a

vague but intense dream. She was walking knee deep in snow in some sort of forest. Her brother was there, but he was so far ahead he was almost out of her eyeline. She was trying to get him to turn around, but he wouldn't. Then, she woke up.

She wasn't sure what to make of the dream, but eventually, her thoughts turned to her father, and one of the last nights they had spent together. The night before he was deployed, they'd celebrated Christmas early. It was a perfect day. They'd made cinnamon rolls in the morning, they listened to Christmas music on the radio, and they even went sledding again. Shortly after Sean and Rosalie lay down in bed that night, there was a knock at the door.

Jim cracked the door open and saw that they were both awake. "Can I come in?" He asked. He had his hand behind his back.

They nodded. He closed the door and went to kneel down next to his children. "I know," he said in a soft voice, "that we celebrated Christmas earlier, but I have more presents for you."

"More presents?" Rosalie asked.

Jim smiled and revealed what he was holding behind his back. It was a small bag, with two small boxes wrapped in tissue paper. He handed one to Sean and one to Rosalie. "Now, these are for you to put away for a while, and wear when you're older."

Rosalie opened hers. It was a silver necklace with a simple diamond pendant. "Daddy, it's beautiful."

Jim smiled sadly and stroked his daughter's cheek.

Sean had opened his now. A nice watch. He looked at it in awe. "Thank you, Dad," he said.

Jim bit his lip. "I love you both so much."

Lying alone in her room now, Rosalie felt the memory slipping, and she fought desperately to hold onto it.

"I don't want you to go," Rosalie told her father.

"I know, pumpkin," he responded.

Jim told them that they had better get some sleep, because they had to wake up early the next morning. Rosalie pleaded for him to stay a little while longer, and he relented.

"Tell us a story," Rosalie said.

"What do you want to hear?"

"About how you first met Mommy."

Jim laughed. "I've told that one so many times."

"But it's my favorite."

He turned to Sean. "What do you say?"

"Sure," said Sean.

"Well," Jim said. He took a breath, and his look grew distant. He was in that other time and place. "When I first met Mommy, things were very bad. Nobody had money or anything to eat. I was living in the city on my own, just trying to get by. There are these places called soup kitchens for people who couldn't afford to eat. When I met Mommy, there were a lot of them. I was waiting in line one day, and I saw her behind me. She was the most beautiful girl I'd ever seen. I knew right away she was the one I was going to marry. I wanted to talk to her, but I was too scared. But we did anyway. And I asked her to go dancing with me. I was so happy when she said yes. And then we fell in love and got married and had you."

Jim lingered for a while before he eventually left.

The next morning, they'd driven out to the army base and said goodbye. Alison cried the whole time, and again, Jim tried to be strong for her.

Rosalie got dressed and ready for school the next morning without having slept much. Her mother was not awake as she usually was to make them breakfast. Rosalie found herself craving coffee, but she didn't really know how to make it and didn't have the time to figure it out, so she poured herself a glass of orange juice and made a piece of toast to go with it, and ate in silence.

As she did, she found herself thinking about Mark and if she would see him again. Since he was a senior, they didn't have any classes together, and the next meeting of the paper would not be for another week. But maybe she'd see him in the halls. Ever since they'd talked at the diner, she'd thought about him constantly. Sometimes, she'd just rest on the image of his face in her mind, and imagine that they were dancing or driving down the road at night or sipping shakes together or any of the other things that couples were supposed to do. He had to at least somewhat feel the same way about her, otherwise, she didn't know if he would spend as much time as he did talking to her.

The feelings both excited Rosalie and made her nervous. She'd had somewhat of an infatuation with Robert Walker, and another with Jack Pickford that had started when her mother introduced her to the silent films she'd loved as a girl. But the former was married and the latter had been dead for seventeen years. The only time she'd ever even come close to having something real was with Ben, a boy in her first-grade class who told her at lunch he wanted to marry her and then changed his mind by the end of the day.

Rosalie often wondered if anyone would love her that way. She saw it so often around her, and it seemed like such a given thing in life that not having it frustrated her. And no one could tell her that she was too young because there were girls her age getting married. Her mother had only been two years older than her when she'd met her father.

She didn't know what she was going to do if this didn't work out. Being alone and having no one to talk to exhausted her.

5

ON FRIDAY, Rosalie found herself drifting off in Math. It was just her luck that they'd place her least favorite subject as her last class of the day—the final barrier before she'd be able to go home. She was especially anxious that afternoon as Sean had invited her to visit his apartment after school. She had not seen him since the wedding. He'd asked to speak with her one day when he'd called their mother and explained that he wanted to see her. So that must have meant he didn't completely hate her. Maybe he wanted things to be better just as much as she did.

The class finally ended, and Rosalie gathered her things. Groups of friends clustered around lockers and water fountains as she walked invisibly through the halls. She let herself drift to thoughts of Mark. Being his steady. Driving somewhere in his car. Walking through the halls with her arm around his, so everyone knew that they were together.

She opened the front door and walked out into the

schoolyard. It was a cold but sunny day, and multicolored leaves were beginning to cake the ground.

It was then that she caught eyes with Mark, sitting on a bench and reading. This time, *A Tale of Two Cities*.

"Finished Gatsby?" she asked, though so quiet it was unintelligible gibberish.

Mark looked up and saw her. "Did you say something?"

"Did you finish Gatsby?"

Mark laughed. "Oh. No. Just taking a break."

"I'm going to see my brother," Rosalie said, nearly choking on her words.

Mark smiled wryly in response, but said nothing. He put the book down.

"Waiting on a ride?" she asked.

"Just my mom," he said.

The two of them lingered awkwardly for a moment. Rosalie felt herself starting to blush. Mark seemed mentally preoccupied, and she wanted to leave before she made even more of a fool of herself. "I'll see you later," Rosalie said.

"Alright," Mark responded.

Rosalie sped-walked away so that Mark wouldn't see her cheeks turning hot. As she walked toward the train station, she found herself thinking about all of the interactions they'd had since that late summer day at the diner. If something was going to happen between her and Mark, wouldn't it have happened by now?

On the train, Rosalie let herself fall into another daydream. She started to wonder what her life would be like not as a girl of sixteen but a woman of twenty-six.

Ten years in the future. 1960. It felt so far away, so distant, nowhere close to being real. She wondered what she'd look like then. Future Rosalie had a glow that present one did not. She lived in New Rochelle with her husband and two children. The girl would be called Caroline. The boy Robert. They were her favorite names of late. Caroline Grace and Robert Franklin, if she had to pick middle names.

Caroline Grace Copeland sounded nice.

Rosalie caught the intrusive thought and sighed. She really couldn't stop thinking about Mark. She was afraid of loving him, although it might have been too late for that.

She turned her attention to the changing buildings. Some old ones hung on, but they were mostly new. It had been nearly eighty years since a fire had engulfed much of the city. Rosalie remembered reading about it in a book she'd gotten last summer at the library. She'd tried telling a classmate in school about it once, and they'd made their disinterest clear. Sometimes Rosalie felt like she was the only one her age who cared about history, about a time before now.

She scanned the train car. Most people were buried in their newspapers.

It was only a few more stops. She remembered. Go straight for three blocks, then left two blocks on Augusta. Number 27. The red building. Apartment 2A. Rosalie approached the door and swallowed when she saw "Sean and Laura Hastings" on their mailbox.

Laura Hastings. Rosalie was never going to be able to get used to that. She rang the buzzer, and soon, she was let in. She felt herself shaking as she ascended the stairs.

What was the big deal? This was her brother, after all. No reason to be so nervous. She knocked at the door. Sean answered. He looked out of sorts, and visibly older than he had been a mere month before.

"Hi, Rosalie," he said.

She smiled. "Hi."

"Come in."

She went inside, and he closed the door after her. Per his request, she hung her backpack on a hook at the closet door. She looked around. It was a tiny place. Laura's paintings were everywhere.

Rosalie inched her way to the sofa. It was covered in clutter, and there was nowhere to sit. A few jackets. Bags. Scarves.

"Oh, just move some of this stuff," Sean said. Before she could, he came and threw everything on the floor. He saw Rosalie staring. "I'll get it later."

She smiled nervously.

"Can I get you anything?" he asked.

"Water, please." Rosalie sat in the space Sean had cleared for her, only to notice a hole. Stuffing poked out, and Rosalie picked at it with her finger.

"Oh, the couch," said Sean. Rosalie hadn't realized that he was watching. "Yeah, we're still upset about that. It happened the first day we had it."

Rosalie said nothing.

"Where's Laura?" she asked. Sean brought her water and cleared a space on the sofa next to her.

"Work," he said.

"She's working now?"

"At a diner," he said. "We're hoping that it's not forever. But we need to. Since we're not getting help from anyone. Financially."

Again, Rosalie had no idea what to say.

"Doesn't Laura's family have money? Can't they help?"

Sean took a deep breath. "They told us the apartment was the most they'd do."

Rosalie did what she so often did when she was nervous. She averted his gaze, down towards the floor. From what she'd gathered over the years, Laura had a difficult childhood, too. She had two older brothers with whom she'd been very close. Both had been killed in the war. It was one of the things that brought her and Sean together in the first place. Rosalie had only met Laura's parents once, briefly, so it was hard for her to come up with too much of a position on the situation.

Instead, her eyes drifted to a painting leaning against the wall. A happy little girl played on the beach while an older one, who looked suspiciously like Laura, watched her up the shore.

"I like that one," Rosalie remarked.

Sean turned and saw what she was looking at. "That one's her favorite."

"It's personal," Rosalie said. "I can tell."

Sean smiled wryly. Before he could respond, the phone rang. Sean answered, and Rosalie could immediately tell from the way he began to speak that it was Laura.

"Excuse me one second," Sean said. He turned to

Rosalie. "I'm so sorry. Laura got off work early. I have to meet her."

"But I just got here."

"I know," he said. He picked up the phone again. "I'm sorry, I'm going to call you right back."

"She's your wife," Rosalie said. "You see her every day."

"I know. Next time, okay?"

Rosalie slammed her glass down on the table. A little water splashed on the floor, but she didn't care. She took her bag and left without another word. She didn't look back to see Sean's reaction.

On the train, Rosalie couldn't help but cry. She regretted her attitude as soon as she left Sean's house, but not enough to face him again. Besides, it wasn't her fault that he'd initiated the visit only to walk it back after she'd come all the way over. It was times like these when she figured everyone would be better off if she lived alone, away from everything.

Rosalie came home to hear Bing Crosby blasting from the record player in her mother's room. "Pennies from Heaven" again.

It was only about five in the afternoon, and all the lights were off.

"Mom?" Rosalie called, turning the lights on. She approached the door to her mother's room and knocked.

"Mom?" she said again.

"Hi, honey," came a quiet voice.

Rosalie cracked open the door. Alison was under her covers, holding a piece of browned paper in her hands.

She put it aside, on top of a pile of similar browned papers on her end table, and sat up. Her eyes were red from crying.

Rosalie stood there, trying to think of something to say. This was far from the first time she'd seen her mother like this, but she wasn't prepared for it now.

"I didn't expect you home."

"Yeah. Um. I decided not to go to Sean's after all." Rosalie was surprised by how easily the lie came out of her mouth, before she'd really had a chance to think about it, and for no good reason, too. Still, it was easier than trying to explain to her mother what had happened, something she had neither the energy nor the will to do.

"You should call him," Alison replied.

"I did. We decided to meet another time."

"Well, that's good. He is your brother, after all."

"Are you okay?" Rosalie finally said. "You're crying."

"Oh." Alison sniffled. "I just miss your father so much. That's all."

Rosalie sat next to her mother, eying a stack of browned paper on her end table. "Are these letters from him?"

Alison nodded. "I never told you or Sean this," she said. "But he wrote letters just to me, too."

"Love letters?" Rosalie said with a smile. Her mother was forgetting that they came in the same envelope, always two. Alison would take one of them out, disappear into her room, and then come back to read the one he'd written the entire family. Sean and Rosalie had both immediately guessed what was going on, even as children.

After a moment's hesitation, Alison took the letter she'd been reading and handed it to Rosalie. "I don't mind," she said. "You're old enough."

Rosalie could scarcely believe she was about to read something that her father had written that she had never seen before. Her wrists began to shake as she held the paper in her hands.

She recognized her father's handwriting immediately, and for a moment, it was as if no time had passed.

"Dearest," it began. She saw that it was dated November 1943. A month before they learned of his death.

There was a lot about how cold it had been, how alone he felt, how much he missed home, how "I'll Be Home For Christmas" had come on the radio, and it had made him cry. Rosalie scarcely could process any of the letter, as the fact that she was reading her father's own words, and reading them for the very first time after all of these years, was too much. And then came the last few paragraphs.

There is a great deal in life that I would still like to do, and when I come home, I swear to you we'll do it all. First, let's go on a trip somewhere far away with the kids. We never did that. Rosalie would love Hollywood. We could take them to the pier in Santa Monica, buy them ice cream and ride the rollercoaster. I still can't believe we've never taken them to Coney Island. We'll have to do that too. They deserve every happiness you and I never had. I want them to be the happiest kids on the planet. I've taken the pictures you sent me everywhere these past few months. They've given me strength.

I've been thinking a lot too, about when we had it hard and we'd lay in bed, just you and me, listening to Sweet Leilani. Do you remember when we said, one day, when the Depression was over, we'd take a trip to Hawaii? Maybe we can do that too. I think I'd like to be far away from here, as far from this cold, terrible place as one can be. The two of us, on a beach somewhere, watching the stars. That sounds nice, doesn't it?

My darling, I do not know when I will be able to write again. We've been on the move almost every day, and sometimes it becomes dangerous. But soon, we will be together again. I know it.

— Your loving Jim

Rosalie held the paper limply in her hands. For a moment, she was taken back to seven years ago, to a time and place when her father was still alive. He'd have less than three weeks to live when he wrote this letter.

44

He was in Italy when he died, the victim of a German bombing raid. He hadn't seen it coming. Gone, just like that. Rosalie took a deep breath, swallowing tears.

"I want you to know," Alison said, "that he loved both of you so much."

"I wish I could speak to him," Rosalie said.

Alison sat up and looked her daughter right in the eye. "He'd be so proud of the beautiful young woman you've become." She smiled again. "He was so looking forward to seeing the two of you grow up."

Rosalie could scarcely hold her tears back now. "Mom," she said. "Why don't I make us some dinner?"

"That would be very nice of you."

Rosalie got up and left her mother's room, surprised at the moment of affection. She couldn't stop thinking about her father's letter. *I want them to be the happiest kids on the planet,* he'd written. He'd always thought of them when he was away. Why did he have to die? Why did he have to die the way he did? It wasn't fair. None of it was.

Rosalie turned on the radio as she began to prepare chicken casserole. It was one of the few dishes she knew how to make, but she was good at it and figured that it would do. Just then, the phone rang. It was Sean. He apologized for earlier. He and Laura were going to be selling paintings at a fall festival the next afternoon. If she wanted to come, she was more than welcome. Apparently, there was a booth that sold wonderful apple cider. Rosalie told him she'd be there.

It was something.

6

HER FIRST YEAR of high school, Rosalie had been friends with a girl named Martine. She had an older brother, too. His name was Claude. The two of them emigrated from France with their mother and father at the beginning of the war to escape the Germans. They'd left mere weeks before the occupation. They'd lived in LA since 1940 and moved to Chicago earlier in the summer for their father's job.

There were a lot of differences between the two. Martine was Jewish, and unlike Rosalie, classically beautiful. With dark, wavy hair and wide brown eyes, she looked like Olivia de Havilland in *Gone with the Wind*. Between that and her accent, she turned heads wherever she went. She'd been dating a senior at their school. They had a television set in their home in Forest Glen.

Claude was eighteen when Japan bombed Pearl Harbor and wasted no time in enlisting. Unlike Jim, he'd actually made it back. Still, something changed, and by 1948, things still weren't quite right.

Martine confessed this all to Rosalie at a classmate's Halloween party as they nibbled at caramel apples. Rosalie dressed as Snow White, Martine as a witch. It was a warm night, and they sat outside.

"My father didn't even have a choice," Rosalie said. "He barely lasted a year."

"You must miss him," Martine said.

"Every day," Rosalie replied. Tears started streaming down her face, more quickly than she could control. She realized it was because this was the first time she'd ever told anyone about it, talked about it with anyone other than Sean or her mother.

"Sometimes, Claude will wake up in the middle of the night, screaming, as if he's still in the war." Martine was far away as she spoke. "Mother goes to him. I put my pillow over my head and pretend I don't hear." She took a deep breath and continued. "He has no wife, no family. The war took that from him."

Sometimes Claude would be jubilant, like he could take on the world. Other times, he would be withdrawn and depressed. Once, she'd come home from school to find him blasting Edith Piaf on their record player as he sat on the couch, limply staring at the wall.

"He didn't know I was there," Martine explained. "It was as if he was..." she trailed off. "*Un fantôme.*"

"A ghost?" Rosalie asked.

"Yes," she said. Martine wiped tears from her eyes. "Mother's been trying to write our family, our friends...

recently, we learned... not many survive. Mon amie Dominique... *Elle est morte aussi*."

Rosalie's face went white. She barely knew French, but enough to think she understood.

"Sorry, my friend from Paris, she was our age. We wrote for a while at first, and then it stopped. She died in Bergen-Belsen four years ago. Rosalie... my mother... there are days when she doesn't leave her bed. She barely takes care of Claude. I haven't invited you to my house for this reason."

Rosalie had no idea what to say. "Do you ever miss France?" she asked after a long silence, thinking of her own ties to New York.

"Not really," Martine replied. "I was so young when we left."

"Don't you ever want to go back one day?"

"Perhaps," Martine said.

"Martine," Rosalie said. "I miss my father so much. He was a wonderful person. He loved my mother more than I've ever seen anybody love anyone."

"I wish I could have met him," Martine replied with a sad smile.

FOR THE REST OF THE SCHOOL YEAR, THE GIRLS HAD been inseparable. That year, they'd spent Thanksgiving together—Rosalie's family hadn't celebrated in years, and Martine's family had never developed a taste for the tradition. That day, they'd gotten turkey sandwiches from a stand in Grant Park. By chance, *Easter Parade* was playing at a nearby theater, so they went, laughing at the absurdity of seeing a movie about Easter on Thanksgiving.

And as much as Rosalie had loved the movie, seeing Fred Astaire had reminded her of her mother, of the films with Ginger Rogers that had been a staple of the early years of her parents' marriage. And it made her think of all that she did not have, all she'd lost, all the war had taken from her.

It was in the final weeks of the school year that Martine stopped coming to school. For three days, Rosalie had no idea what was going on and had begun to grow worried. Calls to her house had gone unanswered.

Then, on the second to last day, Martine had shown up, sullen, withdrawn and barely holding back tears. Rosalie had seen her at her locker and immediately asked her what was going on.

"Claude is dead," Martine said, barely audibly. She spat out the words in a single breath, as if she wouldn't have been able to say them otherwise.

"What?"

"It's terrible," Martine continued, openly crying. "I discovered him..." She broke down. "I don't want to talk about it. I'm sorry." She walked off, leaving Rosalie standing there, limp. A few days into the summer, Martine called Rosalie and announced that she was moving to Montreal. They'd had a cordial afternoon at a diner the day before she was set to leave.

"Mother will like it there," she said.

"I'll miss you," Rosalie replied.

"As will I," said Martine. She'd given Rosalie her new address. "We'll write."

In spite of their promise to, neither had written a letter.

It was over a year later and Rosalie found herself thinking of her old friend as she rode on the train to visit Sean at the festival. Maybe it wasn't too late. She was dying to know how Martine was doing. But maybe she didn't want to hear from Rosalie. She was probably enjoying life just fine in Montreal, with lots of friends and boyfriends and all of the rest.

She got off at the train stop. She wasn't familiar with this part of town, but it seemed to have gotten colder since she'd left. The sun had been out earlier. Now it was cloudy and gray. That was what it was. She soon saw the festival. It was small. Mostly a few booths for food and artists selling their work. Rosalie realized she was hungry and immediately bought herself a donut and apple cider. As discomforted as she was with the cold, the snack was an immense comfort.

She looked around for Sean. Instead, she saw Laura almost immediately, wearing a long plaid dress that Rosalie supposed was supposed to make her look grown up. But it did not suit her at all. She was staring intently into the horizon, but seemed distant. Behind her were a few of her paintings, and around her, a display of various pencil sketches of people and a stool behind Laura's easel.

As Rosalie walked in that direction, she hoped that Laura would notice her so that she wouldn't have to say anything.

"Portraits, fifty cents?" Laura asked as Rosalie passed.

Rosalie stared back at her blankly.

"Oh, I'm sorry, Rosalie. I didn't recognize you." She managed a tired smile. "You look so much more... grown up since I saw you last."

Rosalie still didn't know what to say.

"You wear your hair differently, that's it."

"Thank you," Rosalie responded.

Then, there was a moment of silence that was probably less than a second but still felt like an eternity. "Sean's just getting lunch. He should be back soon."

"Okay."

"There's this diner nearby. They have wonderful blueberry pie. I wish you would have gotten here earlier. I could have asked him to get you a piece."

Rosalie shrugged.

"Rosalie, can I draw your portrait?" Laura asked with a smile.

"I don't have fifty cents," Rosalie lied.

"That's alright," Laura said. She gestured for Rosalie to sit down. "It's not like I have any customers anyway."

Laura looked at her intently and began to draw.

"You look a little like Kate Hepburn, especially around your eyes."

Rosalie half smiled. She liked Kate Hepburn as an actress, but she didn't know if she wanted to *be* Kate Hepburn. Still, she knew Laura was trying to pay her a compliment, and that was worth something at least.

"I've never been drawn before," Rosalie started to say.

"You have to be very still," Laura said.

Just then, Sean appeared with a to-go bag of food,

breaking their concentration. He acknowledged Rosalie with a slight wave and turned to Laura. "How's it been?"

"Boring," she replied.

Then, he looked back at his sister. "Are you drawing her?" he asked Laura with a laugh.

"I thought she could be a good guinea pig."

Sean gave Laura her food, and she accepted it with a smile. Rosalie stayed very still as Laura continued to draw her. She was curious as to what the drawing would turn out like, but she quickly grew tired of sitting there.

Sean seemed to grow tired of waiting, too, because he excused himself. "I should go check on our knick-knacks," he said. "Someone bought the watch."

"What watch?" Rosalie asked, her expression quickly becoming blank, for she already knew the answer to that question. Sean started away from the booth, and Rosalie got up and followed him. Out of the corner of her eye, she caught Laura's vacant expression.

"You sold Dad's watch?" She yelled at Sean, not caring that people turned to stare.

Sean's face was tight. "It was worth a lot of money," he replied. "Money we needed."

"But Dad bought you that watch. It was the last thing he gave us before he died."

"You think I don't know that?" Sean spat, anger clouding his eyes.

"I'd never even thought of selling the necklace," she said, lowering her voice, suddenly not wanting to be yelling at her brother in the middle of a public park.

"Of course, because you know best," Sean replied.

"I can't believe you," Rosalie said, wincing to try and stop her tears.

"You know what?" Sean yelled. Almost everyone in the park was staring now. "Why don't you leave me alone?"

"Fine," Rosalie shouted back. If what he wanted was space, maybe it was for the best to give it to him.

It didn't make the encounter any less hurtful or embarrassing.

7

ROSALIE DIDN'T RETURN HOME IMMEDIATELY. Her mother wasn't expecting her back until dinner, and she didn't want to endure a confrontation about why she was home so early.

On the train, she purposefully took the route that went in the opposite direction of home, and thought about all of the places she could possibly go. It was a shame that they'd lived in a big city and rarely, if ever, took full advantage of it. She couldn't go to the Pier. It was too cold. There were no movies out that she wanted to see.

Then, Rosalie saw that they were near Jackson Street, and she remembered from one time they'd taken Sean there that it was near Union Station.

Something possessed her to get off and make her way to the station.

In spite of the cold, the city was still hustling this far downtown, and it looked busy. Rosalie paused, not knowing exactly what she was doing or if she really wanted to manage that crowd when she had nowhere she needed to be.

Still, she could pretend.

BLENDING WITH THE CROWD WAS EASY. SHE REALIZED that most people probably weren't paying much attention to her. All that was on their minds now was where they needed to be. They descended a set of stairs and ended up in the main hall.

The terminals were down another level, but Rosalie smelled food, so she darted from the crowd and made her way to its source. There were a few different food stands. She got in line to have some hot roasted peanuts.

Donuts. Hot chocolate. And now, peanuts. Her mother would kill her if she found out how she'd been eating today.

Rosalie found a place to sit and eat them, feeling invisible in the massive crowd. It was times like these where she felt as though she didn't really exist, because so few people paid her any mind. She looked at everyone, all huddled in their winter clothes. It was only November, only the beginning of the long, cold winter. They still had five months, six at the most, before it started to get warm again.

She continued to eat her peanuts. They were delicious, perfectly hot and salty on such a cold day. As she savored every bite, she thought about how wonderful good food was. The moment she finished them, she felt a pang in her stomach and wondered if she'd overdone it with all of her snacks. She stood up and made her way downstairs to the terminals and a massive board that showed all of the departures.

First, her eye caught the shorter destinations. Milwaukee. Minneapolis. Detroit. St. Louis. Indianapolis. Des Moines. Then, she saw the more distant cities. New York. Washington, D.C. Los Angeles. Phoenix. She even saw Montreal and Toronto. Montreal. She could buy a ticket to Montreal, if she had enough money, and see Martine. Rosalie wondered how her old friend was doing, and hoped that she was well. She'd have to write her, for sure.

Rosalie sat and realized she still had her peanut wrapper in her hand, so she tossed it. She knew that even if she did have the money, there was no way she could buy a ticket to Montreal or anywhere else. She had school and her mother to look after. She knew there was no way they could go on a trip together, but still, it was nice to close her eyes and imagine.

She thought about where she could go if she had money and time and was old enough to take care of herself. Maybe, if she was a successful journalist, she would travel the country on assignment. Go to all forty-eight states. Maybe, by the time she was twenty-six and it was 1960, she could win the Pulitzer Prize. By then, she'd be far, far away from here and now, walking into Union Station when she had nowhere to go and because nobody wanted her, not even her own brother.

Rosalie didn't understand why she had such trouble

making friends. She often considered the idea that she was a terrible person, and everyone was too afraid to tell her. But if Martine was popular and beautiful and had been her friend, maybe she saw something more in Rosalie. She could never tell if Mark liked her, but he at least talked to her. And her father had loved her. He'd loved her so much that he'd written to her mother that he wanted her and Sean to be the happiest children in the world. Why did he have to die? Ever since that day, nothing in life had made sense.

Rosalie began to cry. There was no way she would be able to hide it, not in the middle of this crowded place. She did her best to prevent anyone from seeing her, because even if someone asked, there was no way that she would be able to explain it. She dried her tears and started the walk back up. A few stared at her, but no one said anything.

WHEN ROSALIE CAME HOME, HER MOTHER WAS resting, so she went into her room. She had to rummage through a few drawers before she found it, hiding at the bottom under some of her thick winter sweaters. When she touched the black box, it was almost as if no time had passed at all and she was back in that room with her father the night before he left.

Rosalie opened the box and gingerly touched the silver necklace. It was still in perfect condition despite being nearly seven years old. She took a deep breath as she put it on and stared at herself in the mirror.

The necklace fit her awkwardly. It was very pretty,

but something about it didn't seem right. Olivia de Havilland or even Teresa Wright could wear this necklace and look beautiful. She stared at her square face, her too large forehead, and too thick dark eyebrows. She wondered what it must be like to go through life as pretty as the actresses she saw in the movies. Still, she kept the necklace on because it was a physical reminder of her father. She took a deep breath and tried not to cry. She cried too much, she thought, and at the slightest thing.

Her mother eventually emerged from her nap and began to fix both of them dinner. She noticed the necklace right away. "That's very pretty," she said. "Where did you get it?"

Rosalie hesitated, unsure how her mother was going to respond. Still, she told the truth. "Dad. The night before we took him to the station."

Alison smiled tiredly. "I'd completely forgotten about that." She sat down next to Rosalie. "And Sean's watch."

"Sean sold it. The watch."

"Oh," Alison said quietly. "I'll have to talk to him about that."

Rosalie said nothing.

Just then, Alison walked back to the kitchen and continued making dinner. Rosalie went over to the radio and turned it on. The first channel it went to was playing Jo Stafford's "No Other Love," which was a new song she'd heard a few times already. But she was just in the mood for it now, and she let the music transport her.

Rosalie could tell her mother was affected by it, too. As she cooked their dinner, she seemed far away, maybe a little too much.

"Do you want me to change it?" Rosalie asked her mother.

"No," she said. "Keep it on."

8

IT WAS SHORTLY after the first snow when Mark approached Rosalie at her locker. She'd been in her own world, thinking about *Sunset Boulevard*, a movie she'd just seen, how handsome William Holden was in it, and how much she'd like to go to Hollywood one day.

She'd begun wearing the necklace every day now. She'd warmed to it as the days went by, as it was like carrying a piece of her father with her everywhere she went.

"Hello, Rosalie," came Mark's voice.

"Hello, Mark," she replied, catching her breath as she turned and saw him.

"What are you doing on Saturday night?"

Rosalie bit her lip. "Nothing."

"Well, um, a bunch of us are going to *The Nutcracker* downtown. My mom hooked us up with tickets, and we have one more, if you want to come," he said.

Rosalie took a minute to process. "I'd love to," she said. He'd said *a bunch of us*. "Who else is coming?"

"I think the only one you know is Joe," Mark said.

"Okay, cool." She had no idea who Joe was or if she was supposed to, but he must have been one of the twelfth-grade boys Mark often ate lunch with.

"It'll be fun," he said with a smile, giving her a slight wave. "See you after class."

Rosalie leaned against her locker, thinking about what had just happened. Since other people would be there, she wasn't sure it was a date, but he wanted to spend time with her outside of school. That was something.

She'd have to wear her velvet dress. The red one that her mother had bought her the year before, but she'd only worn it one or two other times since then. Maybe she'd even curl her hair.

The whole train ride home, she had a smile on her face.

When she arrived back at the apartment, she first smelled chocolate chip cookies and then saw her mother in the kitchen, smiling.

"Hello," Rosalie said, taking off her coat, hat, and gloves.

"Hello," Alison said with a smile. "You look nice."

Rosalie looked down at her beige sweater and red wool skirt, not thinking much of the outfit. "Thanks," she said, sitting down on the couch.

Alison walked over and offered her a cookie. Still warm. Perfect. "Milk?" Alison asked.

Rosalie nodded. Her mother hadn't been like this in a long, long time, and even if she was pleased, she was slightly confused. "Mom, what's all this about?"

"Wait here," Alison said.

As she disappeared down the hallway, Rosalie finished her first cookie and then scarfed down another from the plate. She realized that Alison had asked if she wanted milk, and still, she went to fix herself a glass. Just then, Alison emerged with a large rectangular package. She saw Rosalie had the milk.

"Oh, I was going to get that for you," she said.

"Don't worry," Rosalie replied.

Alison pushed the box towards Rosalie. "I got you a present," she said.

"What for?" Rosalie replied.

"Christmas, I thought," Alison said. "Let's open it in the living room, but be careful, it's heavy."

Rosalie left her milk on the counter and sat down next to her mother on the couch. She wondered what could be inside the package. She opened it, and screamed once she saw.

It was a brand new typewriter.

Alison laughed as Rosalie took it out of the box. She'd wanted one for ages, but never even thought to ask her mother other than a few offhand remarks about how nice it would be to have one of her own.

"Mom," she said. "How much did this cost?"

"Don't worry about that," Alison replied. "I thought you could use it for your writing, for class, or for whatever."

Rosalie hugged her mother. She realized that she didn't remember the last time she had, and it felt nice. "Thank you. I love it."

"Besides," Alison said. "I got a new job."

"Really?" Rosalie replied. "Where?"

"The junior high," Alison explained. "They needed a secretary in their main office. I start tomorrow."

Rosalie smiled. "Mom," she said. "I have something to tell you, too."

Alison raised her eyebrow.

Rosalie hesitated for a moment, wondering if she was premature in telling her mother about Mark. After all, he hadn't exactly asked her on a date. She supposed she was going to have to say something if she was expecting to go to *The Nutcracker* on Saturday, but she could just say a friend had invited her and not say anything about her feelings for Mark. Still, she'd already brought it up, so she supposed she had to say something now. "There's someone, a boy..."

"Oh, really?" Alison smiled slightly.

"He invited me to *The Nutcracker* on Saturday," she said. "I really like him, but I don't know—"

"Well, if he's asked you out, he's got to like you just a little bit."

Rosalie pursed her lips. She realized that now was her chance to say that Mark had mentioned several of his friends were going to be there. But something inside of her kept silent. She thought that maybe her mother would ask too many questions if she'd said that. She simply smiled.

"Well, Rosalie," her mother said. "I'm sure he's a very nice boy."

"He is," Rosalie replied. "He's the editor in chief of the school paper. He wants to go to Columbia for school. He applied, but he doesn't know if he has been accepted yet. But." Rosalie felt another smile creep onto her face and realized she just was talking far more than she was ever used to, and she wasn't sure what to make of that.

Alison stroked her daughter's cheek. That was when she reached out and touched a strand of her hair, which was now past her shoulders. "I think we ought to give you a haircut," she said.

Rosalie was a bit surprised by the comment, and she said nothing.

"All the girls your age are wearing it short. I think it would suit you." Alison laughed. "When I was your age, we all wore it short too. It's funny how trends come back around."

Even though Rosalie hadn't given it much thought, she realized a haircut would actually be very nice. "When do you want to do it?" Her mother would cut her hair, just like she always had for her and Sean while they were growing up. Because Alison had raised both of them through the Depression, she had to learn how to do such things herself.

"Why don't you put these cookies away for me?" she said. "Put your typewriter in your room, and we'll go to the kitchen. You'll look so pretty for your date on Saturday."

Rosalie smiled wryly, saying nothing.

❧ 9 ❧

HER MOTHER HAD DONE a fantastic job with her haircut. Rosalie's hair now went barely past her ears. The next day at school, people who never talked to her stopped to tell her how much it suited her. Mark found her at her locker again. "Did you get a haircut?" he asked.

"I did," she said.

"It looks nice."

Mark Copeland just told me my hair looks nice, Rosalie thought. *Don't be weird.* "Thank you," she said. She laughed, and there was a moment of awkward silence. "So, what's the plan for Saturday?"

"Where do you live?" Mark asked. "We'll pick you up. Joe has a car. Well, it's his mom's car, but don't tell him I told you that."

"1500 Maple Avenue," she said. "Is that okay?"

"Swell," he said. "Can you write it down?"

"Sure. I'll give it to you at the paper meeting this afternoon?"

"Perfect," he replied. "I'll see you." He waved as he disappeared down the hallway.

Rosalie felt her cheeks flush. Goodness, he was so handsome.

After school, Rosalie sat in her bedroom, lost in a daydream. She couldn't stop staring at her typewriter, at how beautiful it was, if it was possible for a machine to be beautiful, and how it was all hers. She wished she had an assignment for class or for the paper so that she could have an excuse to use it. Then it occurred to her that she could write Martine. She supposed such letters were usually handwritten, but she figured her old friend wouldn't mind and that she could always sign her name in her own hand.

She took a piece of paper from her desk and excitedly slid it into her typewriter, thinking to herself that this was only the first of many times she would do this. She began to write.

Dear Martine,

Comment ca-va? That is still the only French I know. I know it has been a long time, but I hope that you are well and that you are enjoying life in Montreal. I am writing to you from my brand new typewriter. My mother got it for me as an early Christmas present. I'm writing for the school paper now. I suppose it'll be good practice for college and beyond. How are you? Your parents? I can only imagine what Canada must be like.

Rosalie took the paper out of the typewriter and signed her name. She wished she could think of more to say, but she supposed that this would be fine for now. Rosalie realized that she didn't know where she'd left Martine's address, but she put the letter beside the typewriter and resolved to worry about it later.

She got up from her desk and went to lie down in her bed. She was cold and got under the covers, even though it was not very comfortable in her day clothes. Her thoughts drifted to Mark and the performance of *The Nutcracker* on Saturday. She didn't realize how tired she really was, and soon found herself drifting off.

In her dream, Rosalie was sitting on top of a hill, much like the one she remembered from her childhood, except this one was a lot steeper and a lot higher than she remembered. The park was covered in snow, a perfect winter scene, and yet, she wasn't cold. She sat on top of the wooden sled, dangerously close to the edge.

"Are you afraid?" A voice came from behind her. She turned. It was her father, looking every bit as young as he did the day he left them.

"Yes," Rosalie replied. She reached for his hand. "I need you."

"No, you don't," Jim replied.

"But it's not fair," Rosalie said, turning to face her father. She tried to look into his kind brown eyes that had reassured her so much as a child, and yet, his entire face was blurry. "Why couldn't you just come home to us? Why'd you have to die?"

"Everyone does, Pumpkin," he said solemnly. Then,

he looked down at the hill. "Now, do you want me to give you a push?"

Rosalie woke with a start. It was pitch black outside, almost seven o'clock in the evening, and her skin was clammy from having fallen asleep in her clothes. She felt her stomach rumble. She wearily got up and entered the kitchen to find all of the lights turned off. She went back to her mother's door and knocked.

"Mom?" Rosalie called. There was no response, and she figured she must have still been sleeping. She sighed, seeing they had spaghetti and marinara sauce, so she got both out and began to cook. As she did, she thought that it was some combination of the dark and cold that made everything seem especially bleak. As she cooked, she tried her best to shake off the dream. She turned on the radio, but nothing she wanted to listen to was on.

BEFORE LONG, SATURDAY HAD ARRIVED. ROSALIE spent what felt like hours in front of the mirror while waiting for the car that would come to pick her up. Earlier that day, Rosalie had tried and failed to find the little slip of paper where she'd written down Martine's new address in Montreal. She panicked in the back of her mind. It had to be in her room somewhere. She hoped that she would be able to find it, because the thought that maybe she'd lost touch with her old friend forever, and had no way to contact her, was not one that she wanted to sit with.

Still, that mattered less right now. Her mother was

calling to her. "Rosalie," she said. "Your friend is here." Rosalie felt her heart pound. She took one last look at herself. She felt pretty. Ready to greet Mark.

Except it wasn't Mark who was sitting on her couch. It was Joe. Suddenly, she put a face to a name. He sometimes spent a little bit too long looking at her and would often wave or say hello as they passed in the halls, but she'd never thought anything of it until now.

He stood up and smiled as he looked at her. Suddenly, she was uncomfortable. "Hi," he said.

"Hi," Rosalie said.

Alison was smiling at them. Rosalie suddenly remembered she'd never told her Mark's name, so for all her mother knew, this was the boy at school she liked so much.

"Where's Mark? Rosalie asked.

"They're in the car," Joe replied.

They?

"Well, we should probably go if we want to get there on time," Rosalie said nervously, her mother and Joe both making her increasingly anxious.

"I'm going to take a bath," Alison said. "Have fun, you two." She must not have been paying attention when they discussed others being outside in the car.

"Let me get your coat," Joe said. He stepped over to the coat rack and started to take Alison's blue coat rather than Rosalie's red one.

"That's not mine," Rosalie said. Her face was hot. One quick glance at her reflection in the mirror told her it was as red as a tomato. Great.

Joe got the correct coat and walked her out the

door. It was an awkward walk down the stairs to the outside, and Rosalie desperately racked her brain for something to say. "So, have you ever seen *The Nutcracker* before?" she finally asked.

He laughed. She didn't know what about her question was funny, but she didn't have much time to ponder before Joe pointed out his car.

Mark was in the backseat. A petite, dark-haired girl who looked like Ann Blyth was beside him. She was wearing a coat with fur trim and had her hair and makeup so perfect it made Rosalie suddenly feel less than. This girl could have actually been in the movies.

They were holding hands.

He gave Rosalie a wave. "Rosalie, Nancy," he said. "Nancy, Rosalie."

"Hi," Nancy said, showing off a pearl-white smile.

Rosalie felt a ten-ton weight drop in her stomach as she got in the passenger seat, and Joe looked over at her. She looked back at Mark and Nancy and realized what this had all been about from the beginning. It was so humiliating.

Why had Mark never mentioned Nancy? Why hadn't he said what this had all been about when he had invited her? If he had, it might have made the whole thing less embarrassing. Fine. She loved *The Nutcracker* and wasn't going to let this spoil a chance to see it performed live.

Just then, Joe turned to Rosalie and smiled at her again. "To answer your question," Joe told her. "I've seen it once before. When I was eight."

"I saw it when I was five," Rosalie replied. "So it's been a while."

"Joseph," Mark said. "You can get lost in her eyes when we're at the show. I, for one, would like not to be late."

How could she have been so stupid?

About ten minutes into the silent drive, Rosalie became aware that Nancy was speaking to her. She mumbled something as Mark had his arm around her. Rosalie turned around to face her.

"You go to Jefferson with Mark?" she asked, her voice soft and sweet. Rosalie wondered if that was her real voice or just airs she put on to get men to notice her.

"Yes," she said.

"I'm at Whitmer," Nancy replied.

"Rosalie's a great writer," Mark said. "And probably smarter than all of us."

Rosalie smiled and turned to face forward in her seat. For the rest of the drive, she remained intently fixated on the road ahead of her. Every time they stopped and Joe could afford a moment to take his eyes away, he turned to her.

After what seemed like forever, they finally arrived at the theater. Rosalie thought maybe it wasn't altogether bad, but maybe that was because she hadn't had a chance to process everything that was happening yet. Maybe Mark hadn't mentioned Nancy because they weren't steady. He'd realize he actually loved Rosalie, and he'd leave Nancy, then Nancy and Joe could find each other too, so everyone would be happy.

They were seated in the front row of the first balcony, which Mark explained were actually the best seats in the house because you didn't have to see past the back of anyone's heads. She agreed with him, and for the first time, she appreciated that they were at *The Nutcracker* and not some dumb drive-in movie. It said a lot about Mark and the kind of person that he was.

Still, Mark and Nancy were talking, in their own world, and Rosalie remained fixated on the details of the stage, trying not to look at them.

Just then, the lights dimmed, and Joe leaned in close to her. "I meant to tell you this earlier, but you look really beautiful."

"Thanks," Rosalie said.

He smiled and reached for her hand as the lights went down. His hand was sweaty, and all she could think of was how she didn't think this was the way dates were supposed to make you feel. Still, she didn't let it go immediately. She wondered if she was being too quick to pass a judgment on Joe. She remembered that her mother hadn't immediately thought much of her father either.

She lasted until the second scene and the famous march. She'd released her hand from Joe's grasp and watched the dancers gracefully move back and forth on stage to the all-consuming melody. Her gaze darted back and forth from the stage to Joe, Mark, and Nancy.

She didn't even have to close her eyes for her surroundings to blur and to remember one of the last times she heard the music.

Western Union.

December 23rd, 1943.

"Rosalie," Mark whispered to her.

She looked.

"Is everything okay?"

Rosalie nodded. Her heavy breathing and blurred surroundings only intensified. Somehow, she found her way to her feet and darted into the empty, ornate hallway. There, she collapsed onto the floor, where an usher noticed her.

"Miss?" he asked. "Are you—"

"I'm fine!" Rosalie shouted.

The usher took a few steps back and away from her.

She started to heave. She could still hear the music, and she had to bury her face in her hands so she didn't collapse. She saw her mother dropping the telegram into the snow and heard her say, "Daddy went to heaven..."

Make it stop, she thought.

She didn't know what was happening to her, but she knew she wanted anything to make it stop.

A moment later, she heard a voice. "Rosalie."

She looked up and saw Nancy approaching her. Rosalie sat up, wiped her tears, and took a deep breath inward. Of course, she was the one who came.

Nancy got the usher's attention. "Cup of water for my friend, please?"

The usher nodded as Nancy sat next to her. "I have similar symptoms from time to time, too. My shrink calls it psychoneurotic disorder."

"You have a shrink?" Rosalie managed.

"Sure," Nancy said. "In eighth grade, I wrote a poem

about wanting to die, and I explained how I'd do it. The teacher was so perturbed she told my parents, they found my diary... Anyways, we've only just met, we don't need to go into details."

The usher returned with Rosalie's water cup and both girls gave him a quiet thanks. "I just remembered something I haven't thought about in a long time."

"Oh," Nancy said. "Do you want to talk about it?"

"Not really, no," Rosalie whispered.

"Then we don't have to," Nancy said with a smile.

For a moment, neither said much. Finally, Rosalie had the courage to ask, "So, are you and Mark steady?"

"Well, he hasn't asked me yet," she said, blushing. "But it's been long enough..."

Rosalie nodded vaguely.

"How do you like Joe?" Nancy asked with a smile.

"He's very nice," she muttered.

Not long after, they went back in. For the rest of Act 1, she was fine, but even more embarrassed about everything. When they all finally had the chance to talk again at intermission, everyone pretended like none of it had happened.

Mark and Nancy went to the bathroom, leaving Rosalie and Joe. The conversation was incredibly awkward. All the time that Joe tried to ask her questions, she kept thinking about what it would be like when he inevitably asked to see her again. If the thought of going out with him on another date made her stomach a twisted, knotted mess, something was wrong.

On the drive back, what Rosalie was fearful of came

to pass; they dropped off Nancy first, and then Mark. Soon, it was just her and Joe.

He turned on the radio, which played Christmas music almost exclusively. Bing Crosby's new song "Silver Bells" came on, and Joe changed the channel. "Wait, go back," Rosalie said. "I love Bing Crosby."

He did, laughing nervously. "Sorry, I didn't mean to offend you."

What was that supposed to mean? "You didn't offend me," Rosalie said. "I just wanted to listen to the song."

"So," Joe asked. "What are you doing for Christmas?"

"My family usually doesn't do too much," Rosalie said.

"Mark told me your father died on Christmas. I'm so sorry about that."

"He didn't die on Christmas," Rosalie corrected. "We found out two days before. He actually died on November 29th of that year. But Christmas hasn't been the same since."

"I'm so sorry," Joe said. "I hope you don't mind that I brought it up."

"No," Rosalie said. "It's a normal thing to ask."

By then, they were approaching her apartment, and Rosalie wondered if Joe was getting bored with her or getting the hint that she wasn't interested, and wouldn't ask her out again. Still, that was proven wrong after Joe parked the car.

"Have a good night," Rosalie said, her hand eagerly moving to the door.

"Rosalie, wait," Joe said.

She did.

"I've liked you since the first time we met," Joe said. "All this time, I never knew how to talk to you."

Rosalie felt her heart pounding as he leaned in. She just had enough time to process what he wanted and dodged the kiss.

Joe was clearly flustered. "What?"

"I don't like you that way," Rosalie said. "I'm sorry."

Joe leaned back in his seat. "Well, then," he said quietly. "What was all of this for?"

"I don't know," Rosalie said. It wouldn't do her any good to mention that she went because of Mark, not now. "You can't force me to feel something I don't feel."

"I wasn't asking you to," Joe replied, more quietly than before. Then he sighed. He got out of the car and opened it for Rosalie, staring at her solemnly.

She got out and gave him a grim look, unsure of how else he was supposed to react. That had been too harsh, she thought, but there was nothing she could do about it now.

She walked back into her apartment, which was dark, cold, and quiet. Her mother was asleep. As she went and changed into her pajamas and got ready for bed, by the time she lay under her covers, she found herself falling asleep rather quickly. The evening had taken its toll.

❧ 10 ❧

THE NEXT MORNING, Rosalie woke up and went into the kitchen to try and make coffee. She had a craving for it again. Alison was already there. She started making some for the two of them.

"How was it?" Alison asked while the coffee was brewing.

"The show? Lovely. But I don't know if I'll go out with him again," Rosalie said, not feeling like explaining the whole situation to her mother.

"You know," Alison said. "I didn't care much for your father right away."

"I don't think this is the same thing," Rosalie said quietly.

"I understand," Alison replied. "If you don't like him, you don't have to go out with him."

Rosalie nodded. The coffee was done by now, and she had hers with only a little cream and no sugar.

"I want you to be with someone who you really love and who loves you," Alison continued.

"Thanks, Mom," Rosalie said before she went back into her room and closed the door.

For a while, she sat on her bed, drinking her coffee and staring at the wall. She was not looking forward to going back to school on Monday and wanted to savor this day as best she could.

Rosalie spent most of the next morning in her room, staring at her wall.

Joe would tell Mark everything that happened between the two of them in the car. Mark would be upset with her for breaking his friend's heart, and she'd probably lose her friendship with him as well. It wasn't fair.

Rosalie had nothing against Joe as a person, but she was simply not interested in him romantically. It was unfair that now she was undoubtedly going to be made to seem the bad person in all of this. Perhaps her wording had been a little bit harsh, but how was she supposed to apologize now? She didn't know why Mark hadn't said anything to her about Joe and about why he'd invited her to *The Nutcracker*.

Rosalie was still trying to wrap her head around the fact that there was still someone at school who liked her and liked her to the extent that he was afraid to talk to her and that he wanted to kiss her. She wondered if she'd been too quick to pass a judgment on Joe, because it felt like all she did was spend time thinking about how she wanted a boyfriend, someone to call her own. Here, she had an opportunity and she'd rejected it. But she couldn't force herself to feel something she didn't feel. Maybe it was better to be single than to be with someone that she didn't love. Rosalie didn't know if she realized that until now. She only hoped that Joe could forgive her and things wouldn't be too awkward for the rest of the school year.

There was nothing she could do about it right now.

After going into the kitchen to make herself toast— she wasn't hungry for much else—she sat at her desk. She wanted to write something. What, she didn't know. After a moment, she took a deep breath and inserted a piece of paper into her typewriter.

It was a cold October day in 1930, one year after the crash changed everything.

It was her first attempt at fiction. But this was a story that she felt compelled to write. It would be the story of a young couple falling in love at the outset of the Great Depression and raising their two children. The story of her parents. She wasn't even sure where it was going, but she was writing and it felt good. She called her mother Edie Porter and her father Walter Hale. She had them meet at a soup kitchen just like her parents had in real life. By the end of it she'd written five pages and an hour had passed. She set them aside, smiling.

This felt good. Writing felt good. It was almost enough to make her forget about the night before.

That evening, she wanted to get some fresh air, so she resolved to walk over to the diner for hot chocolate.

As Rosalie walked, she was struck by how quiet the city seemed. That was one thing she appreciated about winter. The stillness. She thought about how, further down south, in places like California and Arizona and Florida, it still felt like summer. And while she might like to be in one of those places right now, she remembered reading once about how storefronts in southern states would frost the windows around this time of year to pretend it was cold. Maybe there was a girl her age growing up in the Arizona heat that longed to see snow.

As her father used to say, the grass is always greener on the other side.

It was curious that Rosalie had just been thinking about being somewhere warm, because the diner was playing "Mele Kalikimaka" as she walked in. It made her think about the last letter her father had written to her mother before he died. She shrugged it off, ordered a hot chocolate, and sat at the counter.

It was hard to think that not so long ago she'd first talked to Mark at this very table. It had been summer then, and the diner had been filled with people. That felt like a lifetime ago, and yet it had scarcely been five months. On that day, the diner had been packed with people. Now, it was empty and quiet.

She was thinking about what it would be like to be in Hawaii right now when she heard a familiar voice. It was Laura, of all people. Laura didn't see her. She was with someone. A man that wasn't Sean. Laura kissed the man.

Rosalie's heart was beating a million miles a minute.

Then, Laura saw her. She shared an awkward, uncomfortable look with the man that she was with. Then, she started to walk over to Rosalie, her lips pursed into a tight line.

"Hello," Laura said.

Rosalie said nothing. "Where does my brother think you are?"

Laura turned to her companion. "Go," she said. When he hesitated, she mouthed, *"Now."* He did.

Rosalie became aware that the waiter was passively watching them, probably paying attention but thinking that he didn't get paid enough to care.

When he was gone, Laura gave Rosalie a nervous smile but said nothing.

"Where does my brother think you are?" Rosalie repeated.

"Listen," Laura said. "There's a lot going on. I don't expect you to understand."

"Why not? I'm not a little girl," Rosalie snapped, her tone vitriolic. "Do you love him? The guy?"

"Billy?" Laura was starting to cry. "I don't know. I can't be divorced." When Rosalie didn't respond, she kept talking. "You can't tell Sean about this."

"Why not?"

"Because I'm going to end it," Laura said. "I made a mistake. I love Sean. Just. Don't tell him. Not until I can. Please."

Rosalie wasn't sure she believed Laura. A part of her wanted to, but on one hand, she didn't know what she could do about it right now. A million questions were crossing her mind at once. How long this had been going on? How many times had Laura lied to him?

Rosalie took a deep breath and buried her face on the counter. Out of the corner of her eye, she saw Laura leave.

BY THE TIME SHE FINISHED HER HOT CHOCOLATE AND was ready to go home, it seemingly had gotten ten degrees colder, and her worn coat was definitely not warm enough. Rosalie thought about using the last of her spare change on a cab, but she decided against it. The cold air made her feel alert.

When she got back, her mother appeared to already be in bed, which was for the best because Rosalie wasn't in the mood to talk to anyone. She went into her room, changed right into her nightgown, turned off her light, and crawled under the covers.

She'd only been lying in bed for about twenty minutes when she realized that she hadn't brushed her teeth, and also that she had to go to the bathroom. After that, it was futile to try and fall asleep.

As she lay in bed, she kept having to remind herself that yes, she had seen Laura kissing another man. She thought about whether or not to tell Sean. The answer seemed obvious, but she wasn't sure that he would even believe her in the absence of any concrete proof. And maybe Laura was sincere in realizing she made a mistake and wanting to make things right. Rosalie hoped so, anyway.

Even so, Sean deserved to know.

11

ROSALIE WOKE up early that morning to the sunlight against her face. It was seven in the morning, earlier than she needed to be awake. But she knew Sean went to work early, and maybe she could catch him before he left.

"Hastings," he said.

"Sean, it's me," Rosalie replied.

"Oh, hello," he said. "You're calling early."

"Just about to get ready for school," Rosalie said. Sean didn't respond to this. "Hey," she continued. "Do you want to get together this evening?"

"That sounds nice. Laura has painting class, so I'm free."

Painting class. Is that what she had been telling him all this time? Still, Rosalie said nothing. This was a conversation that had to happen in person. Rosalie straightened her posture and took a breath, finding the energy to continue the conversation. "Okay, where should we meet?"

"Want to come to my apartment around five?" Sean asked. "We can find something to eat."

"Okay," Rosalie said. "See you then."

She hung up the phone before she could say more and took a deep breath. She instantly wondered if she'd done the right thing, and yet, there was no way she could take it back now.

At school, Rosalie could barely focus. By the time lunch came around, she found herself sitting alone. Halfway through her meal Mark and Joe walked by. Rosalie and Joe briefly caught eyes. Then, she noticed Mark shoot her a dirty look as the two kept walking.

Rosalie took a moment to regain her composure before she continued eating. There was a lot that she wanted to say, but she didn't know if anything would make the situation any better. She supposed that she was going to have to quit the school paper now. She thought to herself that she might like not to be in high school anymore. She didn't retreat to her usual fantasy about being a reporter for *The New York Times*. That seemed too esoteric, too much of, well, a *fantasy*.

Who was she to have such a dream anyway? Rosalie knew that the vast majority of people who passed through life would do so anonymously. And a good portion of them probably had dreams the way she did. Rosalie knew she wasn't better than anyone else, and she wasn't owed anything in life. The most she could do is appreciate the blessings she did have. She had her family, as broken as they were, and she had a sense that she'd latched onto something with the way writing made her feel.

By the time that school let out, Rosalie had an hour and a half to kill before meeting Sean, so she rode the train the whole way to his neighborhood and ended up wandering around a nearby park. She thought about the story she'd begun, about her mother, who she'd called Edie, and her father, who she'd called Walter. She had no idea where the story was going, where she'd diverge from the truth and where she'd invent. But she was excited to figure it out. Maybe, once she figured out how to tell her mother what she was writing, she'd ask her about what life had been like in those days. Less about the greater arc of the Depression and more about what it was like to wake up and spend a morning in 1930.

Rosalie was acutely aware that the world had existed long before she was born, and that it would continue to exist long after she was gone. She thought about how what was now simply the present would one day be seen as a period in history. Maybe, in the year 2000, people would wonder what it was like to live in 1950.

The park she was in was small and Rosalie must have walked up and down the same path about a dozen times. She was the only person there and the solitude was nice.

It was getting dark. Rosalie checked her watch. It was only around 4:40. It would take less than five minutes to walk to Sean's apartment from here, and she didn't want to be too early and make him nervous. It was hard to believe it was only December and that there would still be four months at least of cold. The snow, she loved. The cold, she did not.

Before long it was 4:53, and Rosalie resolved to start walking over to her brother's apartment. Now that it was getting closer, she felt her heart pounding in her chest. She had no idea how to say what she wanted to say, how she was going to make the words, *Sean, Laura is cheating on you,* come out of her mouth.

When she finally reached his apartment and Sean greeted her at the front door to the building, his cheerfulness didn't help. He was dressed to go somewhere, which Rosalie was taken aback by because they had not discussed any specific plans.

"How are you?" he asked.

"Fine, and you?"

"I thought we could see *Sunset Boulevard,*" he said. "It's playing a few blocks from here in about twenty minutes."

"Well, I'm kind of hungry," Rosalie said.

"We'll get snacks there," he said. "It'll be fun. I'll get our tickets. It can be my Christmas present to you. I told Laura we'd be at the movie."

"Okay," Rosalie replied. Her heart was still pounding. Now, she'd have to wait to tell him. If she said something before, he wouldn't be able to focus on the movie. She also didn't find it appropriate to get into the fact that she'd seen it already. It seemed like this was something he really wanted to do, and she wanted to at least allow him that.

The movie was just as good the second time around and relatively packed for a random weeknight screening. They'd ordered popcorn, pretzels and candy. Rosalie scarfed it all down and it didn't take long for her stomach to hurt.

"Do you have anywhere to be?" she asked afterwards.

"No, why?"

"I mean, I thought we could get burgers or something," she said.

"Why don't we go back?" Sean said. "We have a couple of hot dogs. We can pretend it's summer."

Rosalie swallowed. Grilling hot dogs in the summertime was something they used to do when they were young and their father was still alive.

When they got back, it was very quiet. All of the lights were off.

Sean called Laura's name. She didn't answer.

Then, he turned the lights on, and they saw the letter sitting on the table. Rosalie stood there as Sean walked over to the letter and read it. Then, he limply sat in the nearest chair with no expression on his face. Rosalie approached him, and that's when she saw the wedding ring sitting on the table.

"What's wrong?" Rosalie asked.

In response, Sean handed her the letter.

Rosalie read it.

Sean,

This is the hardest letter I've ever had to write. I'm afraid that our marriage has come to an end. I have not been happy in Chicago for a long time. I will soon be on a train to San Francisco. This is just something I need to do. Please know that I will always love you. You deserve more than I can ever offer you.

Laura

It took Rosalie what seemed like an eternity to be able to form words. Of all the possible ways this evening could have gone, she hadn't been expecting this.

"She's been talking about wanting to leave for a long time," Sean finally said. "I just... I..."

He crumpled the letter in his hand, threw it towards the wall, and screamed. Then, he started to cry. As she stood frozen, Rosalie didn't know what to say or do. She definitely didn't want to mention what she'd seen the other night.

"Is it bad that this isn't a surprise?" Sean asked in between tears.

Rosalie did not know what to say, so she said nothing.

Finally, Sean spoke again. "I'm sorry, Rosalie. We'll have to do hot dogs another time."

"It's okay," she murmured. "Are you sure..." Now,

Rosalie trailed off, but Sean seemed to sense what she was about to say.

"I'll be alright on my own. I'll call in the morning."

Then, he put her in a cab, sending her into the dark and cold night.

12

Rosalie did not fall asleep until four in the morning. Because of this, she woke up later than she usually did. Around ten, she heard the phone ring from inside the kitchen and her mother answered it.

"I see," was all she heard Alison say. "Well, you know you're always welcome here." Sean said something else. "I don't know. I don't think she's awake yet." Rosalie quickly got out of bed and went into the kitchen before her brother hung up. Alison saw. "Wait, she's right here."

Alison put the phone away from her. "Rosalie, your brother wants to talk to you."

"Thanks," Rosalie said, as if she hadn't heard everything her mother had just said.

"Do you want coffee?" Alison asked.

It took Rosalie a minute to realize she was talking to her. "Oh, sure." Then she put the phone to her ear and talked to Sean. "Hi," was all she could think to say.

"Hey, Rosalie," he said. He sounded tired. "I'm..."

He trailed off for a moment before regaining his thought. "I didn't sleep at all last night."

Rosalie said nothing.

"I got ahold of Laura. She was staying with Frankie."

"Who's Frankie?" Rosalie asked.

"Her friend. Did you never meet her?"

"I don't think so," Rosalie replied.

"Are you sure? I thought we took you out to a movie once. The Bogart one?"

"*Treasure of the Sierra Madre?*" Rosalie said, remembering now. Frankie had been so nice to her that night, telling her they'd have to go and get their hair and nails done sometime. She'd found an excuse to decline. A lump formed in her throat as Rosalie realized, in four years, she could never be bothered to care or even remember about anything or anyone in Laura's orbit.

"That's right. I don't know how you remember all those titles. Anyway, Laura'll be in San Francisco next week. We talked for a long time and agreed to get divorced. I'm going to be home tonight." She could hear him crying. "Rosalie, I'm coming home."

"Sean..."

"It's for the best, right? I'll see you around five. I'll call before I leave." He hung up, and so did Rosalie. Then, she shared a look with her mother. Neither could think of anything they wanted to say. All Rosalie could do was sit down and cup her face in her hands.

That evening, he came, and Rosalie went downstairs to meet him. At around 4:55 she went outside, watching for a cab. After a few minutes, it came. The cab stopped. Rosalie watched as Sean got out of it with a single bag. It was a desperately cold day, and she wrapped her arms around him tightly. He seemed so much older and wearier than he'd been the night before.

As soon as they got up to the apartment, he disappeared into the hallway, and Rosalie heard the door of his old room slam. She sighed and collapsed onto the couch, half expecting Alison to hear them and come out to greet Sean. Instead, Rosalie walked towards the hallway and heard the Bing Crosby record playing from her mother's room. She continued walking and knocked on Sean's bedroom door.

"Yeah?"

"Can I come in?"

"Sure, Ro."

She opened the door and saw her brother lying on the bare bed, in his bare room. His eyes were red.

"How are you?" Rosalie managed after an awkward moment she stood paused in the doorway.

"How do you think?"

The tone of his voice made Rosalie embarrassed that she had even asked. "Say hi to Mom."

Sean sighed, wearily stood up, and followed his sister across the hall. Rosalie gently knocked on the door.

"Mom?"

There was no response. Rosalie began to slowly open the door. She identified the song as "Pennies from Heaven" as she saw her mother. She clutched her blankets tightly over her shoulders but her eyes were open. "Jim?"

Rosalie realized she was looking at Sean and he realized it too.

"No Mom, it's me."

Alison sat up and turned on the lamp. "Sean. What are you doing here?"

"Laura and I are getting divorced, Mom. Remember?"

Rosalie looked over at her brother. Sean entered the bedroom and sat at his mother's side. He was going to have to tell her all over again. Rosalie realized that she was tired and slipped away into her bedroom so that she could rest and give Sean a chance to explain in person and not over the phone.

In her room, she changed into her pajamas. She noticed a half-typed page still inserted into the type-writer on her desk and begrudgingly remembered the history paper that was due at the end of the week. She would worry about it later, but not now. She crawled into her bed and collapsed.

IN HER DREAM SHE WALKED THROUGH TIMES SQUARE. A young man in overalls and a flat cap and ruffled brown hair held his lover, a young woman with sandy hair and ragged clothing, in his arms. They shared a passionate kiss. Rosalie watched them, and she got the sense that she was intruding on something.

"You know I'll never leave you," the young man told his lover.

"What about our children?"

She woke with a start. It was half past seven. She heard rummaging coming from the kitchen. Her stomach grumbled and she stood up and walked into the kitchen, where she saw her mother taking out several dishes. She looked tired, but there was a soft glint in her eye.

She turned to Rosalie. "Are you hungry? I'm making dinner."

Rosalie nodded and sat down at the table. She searched for something to say to her mother, but nothing came.

Without looking at her daughter, Alison finally spoke. "I was thinking tomorrow we could go downtown to get a Christmas tree."

They had not gotten a Christmas tree since Western Union had knocked on their door the year Rosalie was nine.

"Really?" was all Rosalie managed.

"Sean's back, so why not? Let's have a nice Christmas."

Rosalie nodded. They sat in silence as Alison cooked dinner and served the two of them.

"Won't Sean want to join us?"

"Let him be alone right now," Alison responded.

They ate in an awkward silence until Rosalie finally said, hesitatingly, "I had a dream about dad. You were in it too." For a flicker of a moment, there was a sparkle in Alison's eye. But she did not say anything, and Rosalie wondered if she had made a mistake in telling her. After a long pause, Alison stroked her daughter's cheek.

Rosalie bit her lip. She wished, so much that it hurt, that she had more vivid memories of her father. There was sledding. There was storytelling. There was the necklace. There were all the times that they spent as a family. But she had been so young when he left, too young to really remember. She wished that he had never died, that she could talk to him about the movies she saw and everything that was going on in the world. That she had the luxury of worrying about whatever her classmates worried about when she heard them talk about their fathers. She remembered that his hugs were strong, but she wanted to feel his arms around her again. She wanted to show him her writing and for him to tell her that she was going to be a journalist.

Rosalie felt tears. She did not want to cry in front of her mother, but they came too quickly. She was surprised when her mother took her in her arms and began to gently rub her back. It felt nice. She didn't realize how much she needed it.

THE NEXT AFTERNOON, THE THREE OF THEM BUNDLED up and got into their car to go downtown to a spot that they'd found earlier that day in the newspaper. The whole drive, Sean stared blankly out the window.

Alison turned on the car radio and settled on a Christmas channel. Bing Crosby was on, which immediately relaxed her. She'd been in a good mood the whole day. It made Rosalie happy when her mother seemed like she had some sliver of hope for the future.

Rosalie watched Sean. He'd been back for three days, but the incident seemed like so long ago, almost like a dream. She dared not think about it now. Sean's intense stare out the window turned into a loud, ugly cry.

"Sean—" Alison started.

He continued to cry.

"Sean, please. Stop crying."

This did nothing.

"Have some dignity."

"I loved her. We were supposed to be together forever..."

"Sean, it's going to be alright. Let's have a nice time as a family, alright? I'm sorry Laura left you."

As Rosalie sat in the backseat, their words, their raised tones were simultaneously sharp and dulled into the background. Rosalie retreated into her fantasy future world. She pictured herself again as a writer in New York. This time, the dream seemed more palpable, like it could actually come true in a few short years. So many writers were going there. Her apartment would look over the skyline of Manhattan. At night, the city lights would twinkle like millions of stars.

They arrived and found a spot to park the car after nearly fifteen minutes of driving in circles. It was a small place, with the selection of trees outdoors and an enclosure where Rosalie assumed that they would go in to pay.

Snow was falling lightly as they walked towards the trees. Once they finally settled on one Alison bought them each hot cider from a small stand beside the register. The workers helped them get the tree on top of their car and they began to drive back.

Alison turned on the radio again and even Sean seemed like he was in better spirits.

"Thank you for the cider, mom," he said.

"You're welcome," she replied. As they continued their drive, she added, "I could make cinnamon rolls on Christmas morning, like we used to. If you two would like that."

Sean and Rosalie nodded vaguely. Cinnamon rolls sounded absolutely wonderful.

They got home and put up the tree but resolved that they would decorate it later. Rosalie retreated to her bedroom to write her history paper and found herself staring at the blank page of paper, unable to think of what to write. She'd already wasted four pages writing and rewriting the same sentence. She checked the clock. It was half past ten and she realized that she was hungry.

In the fridge she saw leftover casserole from the night before and began to heat it up. While she waited, she saw Sean approach out of the corner of her eye. "Want some casserole?" she asked.

"Sure," he said.

"I'm just heating it up now," she replied, gesturing towards the stove. Sean sat down next to her. "How are you feeling?" she added.

"Fine."

"How are you really feeling?"

Realizing what she meant, Sean sighed deeply. He was staring at the table as he spoke. "Terrible." Rosalie bit her lip. The past day had gone incredibly slowly, and in that whole time she found herself wishing that Sean would open up to her. But now that it was happening, she had no idea what to do or say.

Rosalie sat opposite Sean and looked him straight in the eyes. "You're going to be okay. I know it."

"What if I'm not?" He said in a flat, lifeless tone.

"What do you mean?" Rosalie asked.

The casserole finished, and Rosalie began to serve them two plates.

"Let's go to my room," Sean said.

They took the food and did just that. A couple of his clothes were unpacked, but it was still bare. "You know, in a weird way, it feels nice to be home," he remarked.

They sat, Sean on his bed and Rosalie on the desk chair beside him. Sean talked as Rosalie listened. He had a lot that he needed to get off of his chest. Laura had called him earlier. They were going to meet at the apartment early the next day to clear the last of their stuff.

"She cheated on me," Sean said. "She told me that on the phone, the other day. I just..."

"I know," came out of Rosalie's mouth before she could stop it.

Sean stared.

"I was going to tell you, the night we saw *Sunset Boulevard*. I ran into her the night before with..." She saw the expression on Sean's face, and thought it best not to belabor the point.

"So, that's why you wanted to meet."

Rosalie nodded.

Sean covered his face in his hands. "She said she regretted it, but I just... it wasn't supposed to be like this."

"I know," Rosalie whispered.

blotchy and red. They all stopped when they saw Rosalie.

"This is my sister," Sean said quietly.

The officers introduced themselves and Rosalie forgot their names in an instant. They beckoned her to sit down, and then they explained. They found a broken section of a bridge, Alison's totaled car, and her body inside of the lake. There was no note.

And in an instant, everything froze.

FOR THE FIRST FEW DAYS, THEIR GRIEF HAD BEEN paralyzing. Sean kept asking Rosalie how she was, but all Rosalie could allow herself to think was that it seemed wrong that their parents would not be buried together. About a week later came the suggestion that they move to New York. Neither could remember exactly how it was brought up, but the more they talked about it, the more serious it became. There was nothing for either of them in Chicago anymore. It was easier than she thought it would be to pull out of school. There were no goodbyes to anyone or anything, but school seemed to matter so little in that time.

A day after New Years, they buried their mother in a quiet ceremony. It was bitterly cold, but the sun was out. They stayed until they were the last two people in the cemetery, until finally they were ready to move towards their car and get out onto the road.

As they packed up their old life in boxes, Rosalie had turned the apartment inside out for Martine's address.

It was gone.

She knew what this meant. They would never see or speak to each other again. *I'm sorry,* she thought to her old friend. *I'm grateful for the time we had.*

THE FIRST LEG OF THE DRIVE SEEMED TO TAKE forever. When they were finally out on the open road, Rosalie watched as the last glimpse of the Chicago skyline faded into the horizon. Then, she turned around and slumped backward into her seat.

After driving for a few hours, they stopped at a diner because Sean needed coffee. They ordered food too, and were both surprised by how ravenous they were, each scarfing down burgers, fries, and shakes. Their waitress must have sensed that they were in pain, because she didn't charge them for the shakes. They got back into the car and drove well into the night before stopping at a motel, and the next morning they got up and drove in silence until the sun went down. It was a few days like this before they got to New York City.

It was nighttime when they arrived. They drove by their old neighborhood first. Their old house was still there, just as they'd always remembered it. There was a new family living there now. They were unaware that, eight years ago, a man led his children outside this very house in the bitter cold of the December morning. He stopped his daughter to tighten her scarf, and they all got in the car, unaware that it was the last day they would ever see him. They were unaware this was the house where their mother once hummed Bing Crosby songs on Christmas morning while she baked cinnamon rolls. One year, she'd snuck tastes of frosting and forgotten to wipe her mouth, so when she kissed Jim, frosting and lipstick both touched his cheek. She'd giggled like a teenager and Jim looked back at her as if it was the first time they met.

All of that was a memory. Still, Rosalie knew this was how she'd always remember her mother. Not the woman who lived each day in silent torment, the woman who was never fully there, but the one who had everything she could ever want and need.

EPILOGUE

1965

"Virginia!" Rosalie cried, taking her cat in her arms before she could walk all over the typewriter.

Virginia gave her a curious look as Rosalie deposited her on the floor, tossing her favorite catnip salmon toy into her mouth. That ought to keep her occupied.

Rosalie sighed and looked out at the snow swirling in the black night. Knowing Sean, Helen, and the kids were on the road, she hoped they would arrive safely. She took the moment to stand up and turn up the volume on her record player.

After a year and a half of her oldest niece's begging, Rosalie had taken the fact that The Beatles had a new album out—*Rubber Soul*—as an opportunity to listen. She wasn't sure what to make of the album at first. She'd heard "I Want To Hold Your Hand" on the radio many times and didn't see what made the band so special. She supposed being in her thirties now made her a curmudgeon, but she still preferred Bing Crosby. Besides, she'd never seen the appeal of going to a concert to hear nothing but screams.

But the song playing now was striking. She looked at the record. This one was called "In My Life."

Rosalie just had to sit and listen. For the first time, she got The Beatles.

Tears formed in her eyes as her gaze drifted to the framed letter beside her desk.

```
July 29th, 1960


Dear Ms. Hastings,


Thank you for your submission of "The
Edge of Eden" to Starlight Magazine.
Our editorial staff was deeply moved
by your work, and we would be honored
to include it in our upcoming issue.
Our payments begin at $50. We look
forward to your reply as we'd love to
move forward as soon as possible.
```

"The Edge of Eden." The story of her parents. She'd finally finished it after graduating from Barnard. The day someone took a chance on it was the day her life changed forever. She was hardly a literary superstar, but as a regular contributor to the magazine, she got to write. As a night school teacher, she got to instill her love of the craft in others. That's what mattered.

At first, she thought publishing the story would be what she needed to finally put the past behind her. But it never really left her. It was all leading to this new project. One that wasn't fictionalized, but simply the unvarnished truth.

She ran her hand down the edges of the typewriter, remembering with crystal clarity the day her mother had first surprised her with it. It was rusting, the keys got stuck and it smudged easily. Andrew had picked a fight about it in the days before he left.

"How are we supposed to build a life together if you're stuck in the past?" he'd said. "It's a machine, Rose, and machines break down."

It had been four months since their engagement ended, and even though they'd been on a downward trajectory for a while, Rosalie sometimes wished they were still together. They'd met at a time that Rosalie had resigned herself to spinsterhood. Even when things were challenging, being with him had often been simpler and easier than the loneliness and uncertainty of still being unmarried in her thirties.

Rosalie smiled as she saw Virginia perched underneath the Christmas tree, still occupied with her catnip salmon. Rather than despair at the fact that she'd likely never marry, she was content. She had a newfound purpose. She was an aunt to Margaret and Henry. She was going to tell the story of her family.

She took out the pages she'd just written and read them.

In beginning this book project, I often wondered what right I have to be writing a memoir. My experience of World War II and its aftermath was not unique, especially in terms of my generation. Time and age have taught me that, if anything, my life has thus far been profoundly ordinary. These days, I'm often asked about what I'll refer to as the Chicago years of my life, and I have not quite known what to say about them until now.

Much discourse of the last two decades surrounding the "home front" has centered on the traumas of our veterans. This is important work that should be undergone by individuals more knowledgeable than myself.

I do not intend to offer an all-encompassing work, merely, my family's story. The further we get from the post-war years, the more I fear that they will be forgotten. It's not only an issue of the collective, but also, my own memory. The matters that concerned my youth that once felt so potent are mere wisps. As I do not want them to fade altogether, all I can do is write them down while I'm still in good health and spirits.

For now, they'd do.

Sean, Helen, and the kids arrived a short time later. As they ate Christmas dinner, Margaret was incredibly excited that Rosalie had finally listened to The Beatles.

"Who's your favorite?" Margaret asked her.

"I don't know yet," Rosalie said.

"Mine's George. He's so handsome. You have to listen to *A Hard Day's Night* and *Beatles for Sale* next."

Rosalie exchanged a smile with her brother and sister-in-law. Margaret was thirteen now, and quite the extrovert. It was impossible not to see Alison in her eyes, face shape, and sandy brown hair. As the years passed, she wondered if the resemblance would only grow.

"How's the book coming, Rose?" Sean asked.

"I have the preface done," she said.

"What book?" Henry asked.

"I'm writing about the years your father and I lived in Chicago with *our* mother," Rosalie said.

"Grandma Alison, right?" Margaret asked.

"That's right," Sean told her, stroking her cheek.

"I have some albums after we're done with dinner. We could look at pictures. I think some even have Grandpa Jim."

"I've seen them," Margaret said.

"You can look at them again," Helen told her wryly. "We'll all look at them together."

By the time her family left, Rosalie couldn't have felt closer to the past. It was just after eleven when she found her way back to the living room, her typewriter, and the window. It had stopped snowing, and below her was a simple view of the New York streets. She took a deep breath and began to type.

ACKNOWLEDGMENTS

The Hastings family has been in my head since I was fourteen. They, and Rosalie most of all, have grown and changed as I have. For much of that time, I doubted that I would ever get the opportunity to bring their full story out into the world. As such, it is an honor to finally do so.

Thank you to the Make Your Story Matter community for breathing new life into this book through your thoughtful feedback.

To my grandmother, Judy, for inspiring my love of history, the past, and storytelling.

To Kaitlynn Flint, thank you as always for your thoughtful feedback on my work. I always enjoy our collaborations.

Finally, to my readers, thank you for sticking with me all this time.

ABOUT THE AUTHOR

Eleanor Wells is a writer, filmmaker, and actress, born and raised in Milwaukee, Wisconsin. She graduated from Emerson College in 2017 with a BA in Media Arts Production. She resides in Los Angeles, California, and is the author of *All Our Yesterdays* and *Fairytale*.

www.ingramcontent.com/pod-product-compliance
Lightning Source LLC
Chambersburg PA
CBHW050418110726
47899CB00008B/2759